Amarilly Of Clothes-Line Alley

Belle Kanaris Maniates

AMARILLY OF CLOTHES-LINE ALLEY
CHAPTER I

The tiny, trivial touch of Destiny that caused the turn in Amarilly's fate-tide came one morning when, in her capacity as assistant to the scrub ladies at the Barlow Stock Theatre, she viewed for the first time the dress rehearsal of A Terrible Trial. Heretofore the patient little plodder had found in her occupation only the sordid satisfaction of drawing her wages, but now the resplendent costumes, the tragedy in the gestures of the villain, the languid grace of Lord Algernon, and the haughty treble of the leading lady struck the spark that fired ambition in her sluggish breast.

"Oh!" she gasped in wistful-voiced soliloquy, as she leaned against her mop-stick and gazed aspiringly at the stage, "I wonder if I couldn't rise!"

"Sure thing, you kin!" derisively assured Pete Noyes, vender of gum at matinées. "I'll speak to de maniger. Mebby he'll let youse scrub de galleries."

Amarilly, case-hardened against raillery by reason of the possession of a multitude of young brothers, paid no heed to the bantering scoffer, but resumed her work in dogged dejection.

"Say, Mr. Vedder, Amarilly's stage-struck!" called Pete to the ticket- seller, who chanced to be passing.

The gray eyes of the young man thus addressed softened as he looked at the small, eager face of the youngest scrubber.

"Stop at the office on your way out, Amarilly," he said kindly, "and

I'll give you a pass to the matinée this afternoon."

Amarilly's young heart fluttered wildly and sent a wave of pink into her pale cheeks as she voiced her gratitude.

She was the first to enter when the doors opened that afternoon, and she kept close to the heels of the usher.

"He ain't agoin' to give me the slip," she thought, keeping wary watch of his lithe form as he slid down the aisle.

In the blaze of light and blare of instruments she scarcely recognized her workaday environment.

"House sold out!" she muttered with professional pride and enthusiasm as the signal for the raising of the curtain was given. "Mebby I'd orter give up my seat so as they could sell it."

There was a moment's conflict between the little scrubber's conscience and her newly awakened desires.

"I ain't agoin' to, though," she decided. And having so determined, she gave her conscience a shove to the remotest background, yielding herself to the full enjoyment of the play.

The rehearsal had been inspiring and awakening, but this, "the real thing," as Amarilly appraised it, bore her into a land of enchantment. She was blind and deaf to everything except the scenes enacted on the stage. Only once was her passionate attention distracted, and that was when Pete in passing gave her an emphatic nudge and a friendly grin as he munificently bestowed upon her a package of gum. This she instantly pocketed "fer the chillern."

At the close of the performance Amarilly sailed home on waves of excitement. She was the eldest of the House of Jenkins, whose scions, numbering eight, were all wage-earners save Iry, the baby. After school hours Flamingus was a district messenger, Gus milked the grocer's cow, Milton worked in a shoe-shining establishment, Bobby and Bud had paper routes, while Cory, commonly called "Co," wiped dishes at a boarding-house. Notwithstanding all these contributions to the family revenue, it became a sore struggle for the widow of Americanus Jenkins to feed and clothe such a numerous brood, so she sought further means of maintenance.

"I've took a boarder!" she announced solemnly to Amarilly on her return from the theatre. "He's a switchman and I'm agoin' to fix up the attic fer him. I don't jest see how we air agoin' to manage about feedin' him. Thar's no room to the table now, and thar ain't dishes enough to go around, but you're so contrivin' like, I thought you might find out a way." Memories of the footlights were temporarily banished upon hearing this wonderful intelligence. A puzzled pucker came between the brows of the little would-be prima donna and remained there until at last the exigency was triumphantly met.

"I hev it, ma! When's he comin'?"

"To-morrer fer breakfast."

"Then we must rayhearse to-night afore we kin put it on right. Come, all you-uns, to the kitchen table."

The Jenkins children, accustomed to the vernacular of the profession, were eager to participate in a rehearsal, and they scampered boisterously to the kitchen precincts. Amarilly, as stage director, provided seats at the table for herself, her mother, Flamingus, Gus, the baby, and the Boarder, the long-suffering, many-rôled family cat personating the latter as understudy. Behind their chairs, save those occupied by the Boarder and the baby, were stationed Milton, Bobby, Bud, and Cory. This outer row, Amarilly explained, was to be fed from the plates of their elders with food convenient as was Elijah by the Scriptural ravens. This plan lifted the strain from the limited table appointments, but met with opposition from the outpost who rebelled against their stations.

"I ain't agoin' to stand behind Flam or Gus," growled Milton. "I won't stand no show fer grub at all."

"I ain't, neither," and "Nit fer me!" chorused the near twins, Bobby and Bud.

"I want to set at the table and eat like folks!" sobbed Cory.

Mrs. Jenkins advocated immediate surrender, but the diplomatic little general, whose policy was pacification, in shrill, appealing voice reassured and wheedled the young mutineers back into the ranks.

"It's the only way we can take a boarder," she persuaded, "and if we git him, we'll hev more to eat than jest hot pertaters and bread and gravy. Thar'll be meat, fresh or hotted up, onct a day, and pie on Sundays."

The deserters to a man returned from their ignominious retreat.

"Now, Co, you stand behind me, and when you git tired, you kin set on half my chair. Milt, git behind ma, and Bud and Bobby, stand back of Flamingus and Gus. If they don't divvy up even they'll hev to change places with you. Now, to places!" This conciliatory arrangement proving satisfactory, supper was served on the new plan with numerous directions and admonitions from Amarilly.

"No self-helpin's, Milt. Bud, if you knock Flammy's elbow, he needn't give you anything to eat. Bobby, if you swipe another bite from Gus, I'll spank you. Co, quit yer self-reachin's! Flammy, you hev got to pass everything to the Boarder fust. Now, every meal that I don't hev to speak to one of youse in the back row, youse kin hev merlasses spread on yer bread."

The rehearsal supper finished and the kitchen "red up," Amarilly's thoughts again took flight and in fancy she winged her way toward a glorious future amid the glow and glamor of the footlights. To the attentive family, who hung in an ecstasy of approval on her vivid portrayal, she graphically described the play she had witnessed, and then dramatically announced her intention of going on the stage when she grew up.

"You kin do it fine, Amarilly," said the mother admiringly.

"And we-uns kin git in free!" cried Bobby jubilantly. In the morning the Boarder, a pleasant-voiced, quiet-faced man with a look of kindliness about his eyes and mouth, made his entrance into the family circle. He commended the table arrangements, praised the coffee, and formed instantaneous friendships with the children. All the difficulties of the cuisine having been smoothed over or victoriously met, Amarilly went to the theatre with a lightened heart. When Mr. Vedder came up to her and asked how she had enjoyed the performance, she felt emboldened to confide to him her professional aspirations.

The young ticket-seller did not smile. There was nothing about this diligent, ill-fed, little worker that appealed to his sense of humor.

"It will be a long time yet, Amarilly, before you can go on the stage," he counselled. "Besides, you know the first thing you must have is an education."

Amarilly sighed hopelessly.

"I can't git to go to school till the boys hev more larnin'. I hev to work here mornin's and help ma with the washin's in the arternoon. Mebby, arter a little, I kin git into some night-school." A stage-hand working near by overheard this conversation and displayed instant interest in the subject of Amarilly's schooling.

"Couldn't you git off Saturday arternoons?" he asked.

"Yes, I could do that," assured Amarilly eagerly. "Is thar a Saturday arternoon school?"

"Yes," replied the man. "There is a church guild, St. Mark's, that has a school. My little gal goes. She larns sewin' and singin' and waitin' on table and such like. You'd better go with her to-morrow."

"I kin sew now," said Amarilly, repeating this conversation to the family circle that night, "and I'd like to sing, fer of course I'll hev to when I'm on the stage, but I git enough waitin' on table to hum. I'd ruther larn to read better fust of all."

"I ain't much of a scholar," observed the Boarder modestly, "but I can learn you readin', writin', and spellin' some, and figgerin' too. I'll give you lessons evenin's."

"We'll begin now!" cried the little tyro enthusiastically.

The Boarder approved this promptness, and that night gave the first lesson from Flamingus's schoolbooks.

The next morning Amarilly proudly informed the ticket-seller that her education had begun. She was consequently rather lukewarm in regard to the Guild school proposition, but the little daughter of the stagehand pictured the school and her teacher in most enticing fashion.

"You kin be in our class," she coaxed persuasively. "We hev a new teacher. She's a real swell and wears a diamon' ring and her hair is more yaller than the wig what the play lady wears. She bed us up to her house to a supper last week, and thar was velvit carpits and ice-cream and lots of cake but no pie."

Amarilly's curiosity was aroused, and her red, roughened hand firmly grasped the confiding one of her little companion as she permitted herself to be led to the Guild school.

CHAPTER II

The teacher at the Guild was even more beautiful than Amarilly's fancy, fed by the little girl's vivid description, had pictured.

"Her hair ain't boughten," decided the keen-eyed critic as she gazed adoringly at the golden braids crowning the small head. The color of her eyes was open to speculation; when they had changed from gray to green, from green to hazel, and from hazel to purple, Amarilly gave up the enigma. The color of her complexion changed, too, in the varying tints of peaches.

"I do b'lieve she ain't got no make-up on," declared Amarilly wonderingly.

The little daughter of the stage-hand had not overappraised the diamond.

It shone resplendent on a slender, shapely hand.

"Miss King, I've brung a new scholar," introduced the little girl importantly. "She's Amarilly."

As she glanced at her new pupil, the young teacher's eyes brightened with spontaneous interest, and a welcoming smile parted her lips.

"I'm glad to see you, Amarilly. Here's a nice little pile of blue carpet rags to sew and make into a ball. When you have made a lot of balls I'll have them woven into a pretty blue rug for you to take home and keep."

"For the Boarder's room!" thought Amarilly joyously, as she went at her work with the avidity that marked all her undertakings.

Presently a small seamstress asked for instruction as to the proper method of putting the strips together. The fair face of the young teacher became clouded for a moment, and she was unmistakably confused. Her wavering, dubious glance fell upon Amarilly sitting tense and upright as she made quick, forceful, and effective stabs with her needle, biting her thread vigorously and resonantly. The stitches were microscopic and even; the strips symmetrically and neatly joined.

The teacher's face cleared as she saw and seized her avenue of escape.

"You may all," she directed, "look at Amarilly's work and sew the strips just as she does. Hers are perfect."

Amarilly's wan little face brightened, and she proceeded to show the children how to sew, bringing the same ease and effectiveness into her tutoring that she displayed when instructing her brothers and Cory.

The sewing lesson continued for an hour. Then the children sang songs to a piano accompaniment, and there followed a lesson in cooking and the proper setting of a table. All this instruction was succeeded by an informal chat.

"I want you all to tell me what you are going to do when you grow to be women," said Miss King.

In most cases the occupations of their parents were chosen, and the number of washerwomen, scrubbers, and seamstresses in embryo was appalling.

"And you, Amarilly?" she asked, addressing the new pupil last of all.

Amarilly's mien was lofty, her voice consequential, as she replied in dramatic dénouement:

"I'm goin' on the stage!"

The young teacher evinced a most eager interest in this declaration.

"Oh, Amarilly! We all have a stage-longing period. When did you first think of such a career?"

"I'm in the perfesshun now," replied Amarilly pompously.

"Really! Tell me what you do, Amarilly."

"I scrub at the Barlow Theatre, and I went to the matinee day afore yisterday. I hed a pass give to me."

These statements made such a visible impression on her audience that Amarilly waxed eloquent and proceeded to describe the play, warming to her work as she gained confidence. The gestures of Lord Algernon and the leading lady were reproduced freely, fearlessly, and faithfully.

With a glimmer of mischief dancing in her eyes, the young teacher listened appreciatively but apprehensively as she noted the amazed expression on the faces of the teachers of adjacent classes when Amarilly's treble tones were wafted toward them. Fortunately, the realistic rendering of Lord Algernon's declaration of love was interrupted by the accompaniment to a song, which was followed by the dismissal of the school.

"Kin I take my strips home to sew on?" asked Amarilly.

"Oh, no!" replied Miss King. "That is not permitted."

Seeing the look of disappointment in the child's eyes, she asked in kindly tone:

"Why are you in such a hurry to finish the work, Amarilly?"

"We've took a Boarder," explained Amarilly, "and I want the rug fer his room. It'll take an orful long time to git it done if I only work on it an hour onct a week. He's so good to me, I want to do something to make his room look neat, so he'll feel to hum."

The young teacher reflected a moment.

"I'll tell you what we'll do, Amarilly. I will buy one of the rugs that are to be on sale at the church fair this week. They have some very nice large ones. I will give it to you, and when yours is finished you may give it to me in return."

"Oh, thank you!" cried Amarilly, her countenance brightening, "But won't you need it afore I kin git this one done?"

"No; I am sure I shall not," replied the young lady gravely.

When they left the building the teacher paused as she was about to step into her electric brougham. "Where do you live, Amarilly?"

Amarilly gave her street and number.

"You must live farther away than any of the other children. Get in, dear; I will take you home."

She had opened the door as she spoke, and the little scrubber's eyes were dazzled by the elegance of the appointments—a silver vase filled with violets, a silver card-case, and—but Amarilly resolutely shut her eyes upon this proffered grandeur and turned to the lean but longing little daughter of the stage-hand.

"You see, I come with her," she explained simply and loyally.

"There is room for you both. Myrtie can sit on this little seat."

Overawed by the splendor of her environment, Amarilly held her breath as they glided swiftly through the streets. There was other glory, it seemed, than that of the footlights. When the happy little Myrtle had been left at her humble home the young teacher turned with eager anticipation to Amarilly.

"Tell me more about yourself, Amarilly. First of all, who is the

Boarder?"

Amarilly explained their affairs, even to the "double-decker diner," as the Boarder had called the table arrangement.

"And what has he done for you, Amarilly, that you are so anxious he should have a rug?"

"He's larnin' me readin', writin', spellin', and figgers."

"Don't you go to school?"

"No; I hev to bring in wages and help ma with the washin's."

"I'll teach you, Amarilly," she said impulsively. "I'm sure I'm more proficient in those branches than the Boarder."

"He sez," admitted Amarilly, "that it won't take him long to larn me all he knows; but you see—" She spoke with delicate hesitancy and evident embarrassment. "It's orful good in you to want to larn me—but he might feel hurt-like if I was to quit him."

"You are right, Amarilly. You are a loyal little girl. But I tell you what we will do about it. When you have learned all that the Boarder feels he can teach you, you shall go to night-school. There is one in connection with St. Mark's. I will see that you enter there."

"I didn't know thar was one fer girls," said Amarilly. "I'm glad thar's a way fer me to git eddicated, fer I must hev larnin' afore I kin go on the stage. Mr. Vedder, the ticket-seller to Barlow's, told me so."

"Amarilly,"—and an earnest note crept into the gay, young voice—"you may find things that you will like to do more than to go on the stage."

"No!" asserted the youthful aspirant, "Thar ain't nuthin' else I'd like so well."

"Amarilly, I am going to tell you something. Once, not long ago, I had the stage fever, but I think I know now there is something—something I should like better."

"What?" queried Amarilly skeptically.

"I can't tell you now, but you have a long time yet in which to decide your future. Tell me what I can do to help your mother."

"If you could git us more washin's," exclaimed Amarilly eagerly, "it would help heaps. We could take in lots more than we do now."

"Let me think. You see we keep a laundress; but—does your mother do up very fine things—like laces—carefully?"

"She does," replied Amarilly glibly. "She kin do 'em orful keerful, and we dry the colored stuffs in the shade. And our clo'es come out snow- white allers, and we never tears laces nor git in too much bluin' or starch the way some folks does."

"Then I'll give you my address and you can come for my fine waists; and let me see, I am sure I can get St. Mark's laundry work for you, too."

"You're orful good, Miss King. This is where we hev to turn down this 'ere court."

The "court" appeared to Miss King more like an alley. The advent of the brougham in the little narrow right-of-way filled every window with hawk-eyed observers. About the Jenkins's doorstep was grouped the entire household from the Boarder to the baby, and the light, musical voices of children floating through the soft spring air fell pleasantly upon the ears of the young settlement worker.

"So this is where you live, Amarilly?" she asked, her eyes sparkling as she focussed them on the family. "You needn't come for the washing the first time. I will bring it myself so I can see all your little brothers. Be sure to come to the Guild next Saturday, and then I'll have the rug for you to take home. Goodbye, dear."

Knowing that she was observed by myriad eyes, Amarilly stepped loftily from the brougham and made a sweeping stage courtesy to her departing benefactress.

"Are you on the stage now, Amarilly?" asked Co eagerly as she came to meet her sister.

"No; but she," with a wave of her hand toward the swiftly gliding electric, "is agoin to help me git eddicated, and she has give me a beautiful rug fer the Boarder, and we're agoin' to hev her waists to wash, and Mr. St. Mark's clo'es, and she told all the scholars to sew like me 'cause' I sewed the best, and I've larned how to set our table. We mustn't stack up the knife and fork and spoon on ends any more. The knife goes to the right, the fork to the left of the plate, and the spoon goes back of it and the tumbler and the napkin, when you has 'em, to the right."

"I do declare, Amarilly, if it ain't jest like a fairy story!" cried

Mrs. Jenkins enthusiastically. "You allers did strike luck."

"You bet!" cried Bobby admiringly. "Things go some where Amarilly is."

Amarilly was happier even than she had been on the night of the eventful matinée day. The electric brougham had seemed a veritable fairy godmother's coach to her. But it was not the ride that stood uppermost in her memory as she lay awake far into the night; it was the little word of endearment uttered in caressing cadence.

"No one ain't ever called me that afore," she murmured wistfully. "I s'pose ma ain't hed time, and thar was no one else to keer."

Impulsively and tenderly her thin little arm encircled the baby sleeping beside her.

"Dear!" she whispered in an awed tone. "Dear!"

CHAPTER III

Colette King was not one whom the voice of the people of St. Mark's would proclaim as the personification of their ideal of a pastor's wife, yet John Meredith loved her with the love that passeth all understanding. Perhaps the secret of her charm for him lay in the fact that she treated him as she did other men—men who did not wear a surplice. And yet his surplice and all that pertained thereto were matters of great moment to the rector of St. Mark's. Little traces of his individuality were evident in the fashioning of this clerical garment. A pocket for his handkerchief was stitched on the left side.

The flowers, the baptismal font, the altar cloth, and the robes of the vested choir he insisted should be immaculate in whiteness. White, the color of the lily, he declared, was the emblem of purity. There were members of his flock so worldly minded as to whisper insinuatingly that white was extremely becoming to Colette King. Many washerwomen had applied for the task of laundering the ecclesiastical linen; many had been tried and found wanting. So after her interview with Amarilly, Colette asked the rector of St. Mark's to call at her house "on important business."

From the time he was ten years old until he became rector of St. Mark's, John Meredith had been a member of the household of his guardian, Henry King, and had ever cheerfully and gladly borne with the caprices of the little Colette.

He answered the present summons promptly and palpitatingly. It had been two weeks since he had remonstrated with Colette for the surprisingly sudden announcement, made in seeming seriousness, that she was going to study opera with a view to going on the stage. The fact that she had a light, sweet soprano adapted only to the rendition of drawing-room ballads did not lessen in his eyes the probability of her carrying out this resolve.

She had met his reproving expostulations in a spirit of bantering raillery and replied with a defiance of his opinion that had pierced his heart with arrow-like swiftness. Since then she had studiously avoided meeting him, and he was not sure whether he was now recalled to listen to a reiteration of her intentions or to receive an anodyne for the bitterness of her remarks at their last interview.

"I sent for you, John," she said demurely and without preamble, "to see if you have found a satisfactory laundress yet for the surplices."

"Colette!" he exclaimed in rebuking tone, his face reddening at her question which he supposed to be made in mere mockery.

"I am not speaking to you as Colette King," she replied with a look half cajoling, half flippant, "but as a teacher in the Young Woman's Auxiliary Guild to the rector of St. Mark's. You see I no longer lead a foolish, futile life. Here is the evidence in the case," holding up a slender pink forefinger. "See how it is pricked! For three Saturday afternoons I have shown little girls that smelled of fried potatoes how to sew. I shall really learn something myself about the feminine art of needlework if I continue in my present straight, domestic path."

"Colette, you cannot know how glad I am to hear this. Why did you try to make me think the laundry work was—"

"But the laundry work is the main issue. Yesterday I had quite decided to give up this uninteresting work."

Watching him warily, she let the shadow in his eyes linger a moment before she continued:

"And then there came into my class a new pupil, poorly clad and ignorant, but so redolent of soapsuds and with such a freshly laundered look that I renewed my inclinations to charity. I took her home in my electric, and she lived at a distance that gave me ample time to listen to the complete chronicles of her young life. Her father is dead. Her mother was left with eight children whom she supports by taking in washing. They have a boarder and they go around the dining-room table twice. My new pupil's name is Amarilly Jenkins, and she has educational longings which cannot be satisfied because she has to work, so I am going to enter her in St. Mark's night-school when she has finished a special course with the private tutor she now has."

"Colette," said the young minister earnestly, "why do you continually try to show yourself to me in a false light? It was sweet in you to take this little girl home in your brougham and to feel an interest in her improvement."

"Not at all!" protested Colette. "My trend at present may appear to be charitable, but Amarilly and I have a common interest—a fellow feeling—that makes me wondrous kind. We both have longings to appear in public on the stage."

At this sudden challenge, this second lowering of the red flag, John's face grew stern.

"Amarilly," continued the liquid voice,—"has had more experience in stage life than I have had. She has commenced at the lowest round of the dramatic ladder of fame. She scrubs at the Barlow Theatre, and she is quite familiar with stage lore. Her hero is the man who plays the role of Lord Algernon in A Terrible Trial."

He made no reply, and Colette presently broke the silence.

"Seriously, John," she said practically and in a tone far different from her former one, "the Jenkins family are poor and most deserving. I am going to give them some work, and if you would give them a trial on the church linen, it would help them so much. There was a regular army of little children on the doorstep, and it must be a struggle to feed them all. I should like to help them—to give them something—but they seem to be the kind of people that you can help only by giving them work to perform. I have learned that true independence is found only among the poor."

John took a little notebook from his pocket.

"What is their address, Colette?"

She took the book from him and wrote down the street and number.

"Colette, you endeavor to conceal a tender heart—"

"And will you give them—Mrs. Jenkins—a trial?"

"Yes; this week."

"That will make Amarilly so happy," she said, brightening. "I am going there to-morrow to take them some work, and I will tell Mrs. Jenkins to send Flamingus—his is the only name of the brood that my memory retains—for the church laundry."

"He may call at the rectory," replied John, "and get the house laundry as well."

"That will be good news for them. I shall enjoy watching Amarilly's face when she hears it."

"And now, Colette, will you do something for me?"

"Maybe. What is it?" she asked guardedly.

"Will you abandon the idea of going on the stage, or studying for that purpose?"

"Perforce. Father won't consent."

A look of relief drove the trouble from the dark eyes fixed on hers.

"I'll be twenty-one in a year, however," she added carelessly.

John was wise enough to perceive the wilfulness that prompted this reply, and he deftly changed the subject of conversation.

"About this little girl, Amarilly. We must find her something in the way of employment. The atmosphere of a theatre isn't the proper one for a child of that age. Do you think so?"

"Theoretically, no; but Amarilly is not impressionable to atmosphere altogether. She seems a hard-working, staunch little soul, and all that relieves the sordidness of her life and lightens the dreariness of her work is the 'theayter,' as she calls it. So don't destroy her illusions, John. You'll do her more harm than good."

"Not if I give her something real in the place of what you rightly term her illusions."

"You can't. Sunday-school would not satisfy a broad-minded little proletarian like Amarilly, so don't preach to her."

He winced perceptibly.

"Do I preach to you, Colette? Is that how you regard me—as a prosy preacher who—"

"No, John. Just as a disturber of dreams—that is all."

"A disturber of dreams?" he repeated wistfully. "It is you, Colette, who are a disturber of dreams. If you would only let my dreams become realities!"

"Then, to be paradoxical, your realities might change back to dreams, or even nightmares. Returning to soapsuds and Amarilly Jenkins, will you go there with me to-morrow and make arrangements with Mrs. Jenkins for the laundry work?"

"Indeed I will, Colette, and—"

"Don't look so serious, John. Until that dreadful evening, the last time you called, you always left your pulpit punctilio behind you when you came here."

"Colette!" he began in protest.

But she perversely refused to fall in with his serious vein. Chattering gayly yet half-defiantly, on her face the while a baffling smile, partly tender, partly amused, and wholly coquettish—the smile that maddened and yet entranced him—she brought the mask of reserve to his face and man. At such times he never succeeded in remembering that she was but little more than a child, heart-free, capricious, and wilful. Despairing of changing her mood to the serious one that he loved yet so seldom evoked, he arose and bade her good-night.

When he was in the hall she softly called him back, meeting him with a half-penitent look in her eyes, which had suddenly become gazelle-like.

"You may preach to me again some time, John. There are moments when I believe I like it, because no other man dares to do it" "Dares?" he queried with a smile.

"Yes; dares. They all fear to offend. And you, John, you fear nothing!"

"Yes, I do," he answered gravely, as he looked down upon her. "There is one thing I fear that makes me tremble, Colette."

But her mood had again changed, and with a mischievous, elusive smile she bade him go. Inert and musing, he wandered at random through the lights and shadows of the city streets, with a wistful look in his eyes and just the shadow of a pang in his heart.

"She is very young," he said condoningly, answering an accusing thought. "She has been a little spoiled, naturally. She has seen life only from the side that amuses and entertains. Some day, when she realizes, as it comes to us all to do, that care and sorrow bring their own sustaining power, she will not dally among the petty things of life; the wilful waywardness will turn to winning womanliness."

CHAPTER IV

The next afternoon when Amarilly came home from the theatre, her mother met her with another burst of information.

"Miss King and the preacher was here. He's agoin' to give us all the church surpluses to wash and his house-wash, too. Flamingus is to go fer them to the rectry to-night, and you're to go to Miss King's and get the waists she has to be did up. She left two car tickets fer you."

"We air jest astubbin' our toes on luck," gasped Amarilly.

"The fust pay from the new washin's shall go fer a new hat and dress fer you, Amarilly. It's acomin' to you all right. 'Twas you as got this work fer us."

"No!" was the emphatic reply. "We'll git some more cheers, knives, spoons, plates, cups, and two more leaves fer the table, so's the chillern kin all set to table to onct."

"That'll be a hull lot more convenient," admitted Mrs. Jenkins hopefully. "Co spills things so, and the boys quarrel when you and the Boarder ain't here to keep peace. It was jest orful this noon. You wasn't here and the Boarder kerried his dinner. 'Cause Flam put too much vinegar on Milt's beans, Milt poured it down Flam's neck, and when I sent him away from the table he sassed me."

"Jiminy!" protested Amarilly indignantly. "I'd make Milt go without his supper to-night."

"'Tain't his stummick I'm agoin' to punish," said Mrs. Jenkins sarcastically. "I've laid by a willer switch that'll feel sharper than the vinegar he wasted. You'd better go to Miss King's right away — and, Amarilly, mind you ride both ways. It's too far to walk. Don't you sell the tickets!"

This last prohibitory remark was made in remembrance of Amarilly's commercial instincts.

When Amarilly was admitted to the basement of her young benefactress's home a trimly-capped little maid took her to Colette's boudoir.

"Sit down and talk to me, Amarilly. I want to hear more about Lord Algernon and Mr. Vedder and Pete. Here's a box of chocolate creams that must be eaten while they are fresh."

Amarilly was slightly awed at first by the luxurious appointments of the room, but she soon recovered her ease and devoured the novel sweets with appreciative avidity. Then she proved herself a fascinating raconteur of the annals of a world unknown to Colette. It was a matter of course to Amarilly that the leading lady should be supporting an invalid sister; that the languid Lord Algernon should be sending his savings to his old mother who lived in the country; that the understudy should sew industriously through rehearsals and behind the scenes between parts for her two little fatherless girls; that Pete Noyes should "bank" to buy a wheeled chair for his rheumatic father; that the villain was "layin' by" for his parents to come from the Fatherland, and that the company should all chip in to send the property woman's sick child to the seashore. But to Colette the homely little stories were vignettes of another side of life.

"Have you been to the rectory yet, Amarilly?" she asked presently, when Amarilly's memories of stage life lagged.

"No; Flammy has went fer Mr. St. Mark's things."

"Mr. St. Mark's!"

Colette laughed delightedly.

"I thought you told me that the preacher's name was Mr. St. Marks. You said mebby you could git his wash fer us."

"No, Amarilly. I did not mean that. St. Mark's is the name of the church where he officiates. He could never under any conditions be a St. Mark."

"Wat's his name?"

"St. John, of course. And most people call him a rector, but really your name suits him best. He does preach — sometimes — to me."

At the end of the week Colette again sent for John — to call "on laundry business" — her little note read.

23

"I couldn't wait," she said when he came, "to learn how Mrs. Jenkins pleased you. My waists were most beautifully laundered. She is certainly a Madonna of the Tubs."

"You have indeed secured a treasure for me, Colette. The linen is immaculate, and she shall have the laundering of it regularly."

"I am so glad!" exclaimed Colette fervently. "They need it so much, and they are so anxious to please. Amarilly was so apprehensive—"

John's face had become radiant.

"It is sweet in you to be interested, Colette, and—"

"I wish you would see her," said Colette, ignoring his commendatory words and voice. "She's an odd little character. I invited her to luncheon the other day, and the courses and silver never disturbed her apparently. She watched me closely, however, and followed my moves as precisely as a second oarsman. By the way, she called you St. Mark. I know some people consider you and St. Mark's as synonymous, but I explained the difference. She tells me absorbingly interesting stories of theatre life—the life behind the scenes. You see the 'scent of the roses,' John!"

The shadow fell again, but he made no response.

The following Monday the young minister chanced to be in the culinary precincts of the rectory when Amarilly called for the laundry, none of the boys having been available for the service.

An instant gleam of recognition came into his kindly eyes.

"You must be Amarilly Jenkins. I have heard very good accounts of you—that you are industrious and a great help to your mother."

Amarilly looked at him shrewdly.

"She told you," she affirmed positively.

There was but one "she" in the world of these two, and John Meredith naturally comprehended.

"She's orful good to us," continued Amarilly, "and it was through her,

Mr. St. John, that we got the surpluses."

"It was, indeed, Amarilly; but my name is not St. John. It is John Meredith."

"She was jest kiddin' me, then!" deduced Amarilly appreciatively. "I thought at fust as how yer name was St. Mark, and she said you could never be a St. Mark, that you was St. John. She likes a joke. Mr. Reeves-Eggleston (he's playin' the part of the jilted man in the new play this week) says it's either folks as never hez hed their troubles or them as hez hed more'n their share what laughs at everything, only, he says, it's diffrent kinds of laughs."

The reference to the play reminded John of a duty to perform.

"Miss King told me, Amarilly, that you want to go on the stage when you grow up."

"I did plan to go on, but she said when I got eddicated, I might hear of other things to do — things I'd like better. So mebby I'll change my mind."

A beautiful smile lightened John's dark eyes.

"She, was right, Amarilly. There are things that would be better for you to do, and I — we — will try to help you find them."

"Every one gits the stage fever some time," remarked Amarilly philosophically, "She said so. She said she had it once herself, but she knew now that there was something she would like better."

His smile grew softer.

"She wouldn't tell me what it was," continued Amarilly musingly. Then a troubled look came into her eyes.

"Mebby I shouldn't tell you what she says. Flamingus says I talk too much."

"It was all right to tell me, Amarilly," he replied with radiant eyes, "as long as she said nothing personal."

Amarilly looked mystified.

"I mean," he explained gently, "that she said nothing of me, nothing that you should not repeat. I am glad, though, to see that you are conscientious.

Miss King tells me you are to go to the night-school. Do you attend Sunday-school?"

Amarilly looked apologetic.

"Not reg'lar. Thar's a meetin'-house down near us that we go to sometimes. Flamingus and me and Gus give a nickel apiece towards gittin' a malodeyon fer it, but it squeaks orful. 'Tain't much like the orchestry to the theayter. And then the preacher he whistles every time he says a word that has an 's' in it. You'd orter hear him say: 'Let us sing the seventy-seventh psalm.'"

At the succession of the sibilant sounds, John's brown eyes twinkled brightly, and about his mouth came crinkly, telltale creases of humor.

"And they sing such lonesome tunes," continued Amarilly, "slower than the one the old cow died on. I was tellin' the stage maniger about it, and he said they'd orter git a man to run the meetin'-houses that understood the proper settin's. Everything, he says, is more'n half in the settin's."

"Amarilly," was the earnest response, "will you come to St. Mark's next Sunday to the morning service? The music will please you, I am sure, and there are other things I should like to have you hear."

Amarilly solemnly accepted this invitation, and then went home, trundling a big cart which contained the surplices and the rectory laundry.

Colette's remarks, so innocently repeated to him, made John take himself to task.

"I knew," he thought rapturously, "that she was pure gold at heart. And it is only her sweet willfulness that is hiding it from me."

That evening he found Colette sitting before an open fire in the library, her slender little feet crossed before the glowing blaze. She was in a gentle, musing mood, but at his entrance she instantly rallied to her old mirth-loving spirit.

"I have made Amarilly's acquaintance," he said. "She is coming to church next Sunday."

"A convert already! And you will try to snatch poor Amarilly, too, from her footlight dreams?"

"Colette," he replied firmly, "you can't play a part with me any longer.

You, the real Colette, made it unnecessary for me to remonstrate with

Amarilly on her choice of professions. She is wavering because of your

assurance that there are better things in life for her to engage in."

He was not very tall, but stood straight and stalwart, with the air of one born to command. At times he seemed to tower above all others.

She regarded him with an admiring look which changed to wonder at what she read in his eyes. In a flash she felt the strength and depth of his feeling, but her searching scrutiny caused him to become tongue-tied, and he assumed the self-conscious mien peculiar to the man not yet assured that his love is returned. Once more a golden moment slipped away with elfish elusiveness, and Colette, secure in her supremacy, resumed her tantalizing badinage.

CHAPTER V

The Jenkins family was immediately summoned in council to discuss Amarilly's invitation to attend divine service at St. Mark's.

"You air jest more'n hevin' advantages," said Mrs. Jenkins exultingly. "Fust the matinée, then the Guild, and now St. Mark's is open to you. But you'd orter hev a few fixin's to go to sech a grand place, Amarilly."

Amarilly shook her determined little head resolutely.

"We can't afford it," she said decisively. "I'd stay to hum afore I'd spend anything on extrys now when we're aketchin' up and layin' by."

"'Twould be good bookkeepin' fer you ter go," spoke up Flamingus. "You see the preacher's givin' us his business, and we'd orter return the favor and patrynize his church. You've gotter hustle to hold trade arter you git it these days. It's up to you ter go, Amarilly." Mrs. Jenkins looked proudly at her eldest male offspring.

"I declare, Flamingus, you've got a real business head on you jest like your pa hed. He's right, Amarilly. 'Twouldn't be treating Mr. Meredith fair not ter go, and it's due him that you go right, so he won't be ashamed of you. I'll rig you up some way."

The costuming of Amarilly in a manner befitting the great occasion was an all-absorbing affair for the next few days. Finally, by the combination of Mrs. Jenkins's industry and Amarilly's ingenuity, aided by the Boarder and the boys, an elaborate toilet was devised and executed. Milton donated a "shine" to a pair of tan shoes, the gift of the girl "what took a minor part." Mrs. Jenkins looked a little askance at the "best skirt" of blue which had shrunk from repeated washings to a near-knee length, but Amarilly assured her that it was not as short as the skirts worn by the ballet girls. She cut up two old blouses and fashioned a new, bi-colored waist bedizened with gilt buttons. The Boarder presented a resplendent buckle, and Flamingus provided a gawdy hair-ribbon.

The hat was the chief difficulty. On week days she wore none, but of course St. Mark's demanded a headgear of some kind, and at last Mrs. Jenkins triumphantly produced one of Tam o' Shanter shape manufactured from a lamp mat and adorned with some roses bestowed by the leading lady. The belligerent locks of the little scrub-girl refused to respond to advances from curling iron or papers, but one of the neighbors whose hair was a second cousin in hue to Amarilly's amber tresses, loaned some frizzes, which were sewed to the brim of the new hat. The problem of hand covering was solved by Mr. Vedder, as a pair of orange-tinted gloves had been turned in at the box-office by an usher, and had remained unclaimed. They proved a perfect fit, and were the supreme triumph of the bizarre costume.

Not even Solomon in all his glory was arrayed in splendor greater than that displayed by Amarilly when she set forth on Sunday morning for St. Mark's. Promptness was ever Amarilly's chief characteristic, and she arrived long in advance of the ushers. This gave her an opportunity to sample several pews before finally selecting one whose usual occupants, fortunately, were out of the city.

The vastness and stillness of the edifice, disturbed now and then by silken rustle and soft-shod foot were bewildering to Amarilly. She experienced a slight depression until the vibrating tones of the organ fell softly upon the air. The harmony grew more subdued, ceased, and was succeeded by another moment of solemn silence. Then a procession of white-robed choristers came down the aisle, their well-trained voices ringing out in carolling cadence.

"Them's the chorus," thought Amarilly.

Entranced, she listened to the service, sitting upright and very still. The spiritual significance of the music, the massing of foliage and flowers in the chancel, the white altars with their many lighted candles, were very impressive to the little wide-eyed worshipper.

"Their settin's is all right," she said to herself critically, "and it ain't like the theayter. It's—"

A sudden revealing light penetrated the shadows of her little being.

"This is the real thing!" she acknowledged.

There was only one disappointment to mar the perfection. She felt quite aggrieved that Mr. Meredith—or Mr. St. John as she still called him in her thoughts—did not "come on" in the first act.

"Mebby he don't hev the leadin' part to-day," she thought disappointedly, as a callow youth, whose hair was pompadoured and whose chin receded, began to read the lessons for the day. Amarilly was kept in action by her effort to follow the lead of the man in front of her.

"It's hard to know jest when to set or stand or pray, but it keeps things from draggin'," she thought, "and thar's no chanct to git sleepy. It keeps me jest on the hump without no rayhearsal fer all this scene shiftin'."

Her little heart quickened in glad relief when the erect form of John Meredith ascended the pulpit to deliver the sermon.

"That other one was jest the understudy," she concluded.

The sermon, strong, simple, and sweet like John himself, was delivered in a rich, modulated voice whose little underlying note of appeal found entrance to many a hard-shell heart. The theology was not too deep for the attentive little scrubber to comprehend, and she was filled with a longing to be good—very good. She made ardent resolutions not to "jaw" the boys so much, and to be more gentle with Iry and Go. Her conscience kept on prodding until she censured herself for not mopping the corners at the theatre more thoroughly.

At the conclusion of the sermon the rector with a slight tremor in his mellifluous voice pronounced the benediction. Amarilly's eyes shone with a light that Lord Algernon's most eloquent passages could never have inspired.

The organ again gave forth its rich tones, and a young, fair-haired boy with the face of a devotee arose and turned toward the congregation, his face uplifted to the oaken rafters. A flood of sunshine streamed through the painted window and fell in long slanting rays upon the spiritual face. The exquisite voice rose and fell in silvery cadence, the soft notes fluting out through the vast space and reaching straight to Amarilly's heart which was beating in unison to the music. "Oh," she thought wistfully, "if Pete Noyes was only like him!"

She responded to the offertory with a penny, which lay solitary and outlawed on the edge of a contribution plate filled with envelopes and bank bills. The isolated coin caught the eye of the young rector as he received the offerings, and his gaze wandered wonderingly over his fashionable congregation. It finally rested upon the small, eager-eyed face of his washerwoman's daughter, and a look of angelic sweetness came into his brown eyes with the thought: "Even the least of these!"

Colette, statuesque and sublime, caught the flash of radiance that illumined the face of her pastor, and her heart-strings responded with a little thrill.

There was another fervent prayer in low, pleading tones, after which followed the recessional, the choir-boys chanting their solemn measures.

Amarilly in passing out saw John, clad in a long, tight-fitting black garment, standing at the church door.

"He's got another costume fer the afterpiece," she thought admiringly. "He must be a lightning change artist like the one down to the vawdyveel that Pete was tellin' of!"

Then two wonderful, heart-throbbing things happened. John took Amarilly's saffron-clad hand in his and told her in earnest, convincing tones how glad he was that she had come, and that he should look for her every Sunday.

"He held up the hull p'rade fer me!" she thought exultingly.

As he was speaking to her his gaze wandered away for a second; in that infinitesimal space of time there came into his eyes a dazzling flash of light that was like a revelation to the sharp-eyed little girl, who, following the direction of his glance, beheld Colette. Then came the second triumph. Colette, smiling, shook hands with her and praised her attire.

"Did you like the service, Amarilly?" she whispered. "Was it like the theatre?"

"It was diffrent," said Amarilly impressively. "I think it's what heaven is!"

"And did you like the sermon St. John preached?"

Amarilly's lips quivered.

"I liked it so much, I liked him so much, I'd ruther not talk about it."

Colette stooped and kissed the freckled little face, to the utter astonishment of those standing near and to the complete felicity of John Meredith, who was a witness of the little scene though he did not hear the conversation.

Amarilly walked homeward, her uplifted face radiant with happiness.

"The flowers, the lights, oh, it was great!" she thought. "Bud could sing like that if he was learnt. He couldn't look like that surplused boy, though. He sorter made me think of Little Eva in the play they give down to Milt's school. I wish Bud's hair was yaller and curly instead of black and straight!"

Amarilly's reminiscences next carried her to the look she had seen in the rector's eyes when he beheld Colette coming out of the church.

"It was the look Lord Algernon tried to give Lady Cecul," she thought, "only he couldn't do it, 'cause it wasn't in Him to give. And it couldn't never be in him the same as 't is in Mr. St. John and Miss King. It ain't in her yet to see what was in his eyes. Some day when she gits more feelin's, mebby 't will be, though."

When Amarilly had faithfully pictured the service to the household,

Bud's anaemic face grew eager.

"Take me with yer, Amarilly, next time, won't yer?" he pleaded.

"It's too fer. You couldn't walk, Buddy," she answered, "and we can't afford car-fare fer two both ways."

"I'll take him to-night," promised the Boarder. "We'll ride both ways, so fur as we kin. I'd like to hear a sermon now and then, especially by a young preacher."

The little family stayed up that night until the return of Bud and the

Boarder who were vociferous in approval of the service.

"It ain't much like our meetin'-house," said Bud. "It was het and lit. And the way that orgin let out! Say, Amarilly, thar wasn't no man in sight to play it! I s'pose they've got one of them things like a pianner-player. Them surplused boys sung fine!"

"He give us a fine talk," reported the Boarder. "I've allers thought if a man paid a hundred cents on the dollar, 't was all that was expected of him. But I believe it's a good idee to go to church and keep your conscience jogged up so it won't rust. I'll go every Sunday, mebby, and take Bud so he kin larn them tunes."

"I never go to no shows nor nuthin'!" wailed Cory.

"I'll take you next time," soothed Amarilly. "I kin work you'se off on the kinductor as under age, I guess, if you'll crouch down."

CHAPTER VI

Monday's mops and pails broke in upon the spell of Amarilly's spiritual enchantment to some extent, but remembrance of the scenic effects lingered and was refreshed by the clothes-line of vestal garb which manifested the family prosperity, and heralded to the neighborhood that the Jenkins's star was in the ascendant.

"Them Jenkinses," said Mrs. Hudgers, who lived next door, "is orful stuck up sence they got the sudsin' of them surpluses."

This animadversion was soon conveyed to Amarilly, who instantly and freely forgave the critic.

"She's old and rheumatic," argued the little girl. "She can't git to go nowhars, and folks that is shut in too long spiles, jest like canned goods. Besides, her clock has stopped. Nobody can't go on without no clock."

Out of pity for the old woman's sequestered life, Amarilly was wont to relate to her all the current events, and it was through the child's keen, young optics that Mrs. Hudgers saw life. An eloquent and vivid description of St. Mark's service was eagerly related.

"I allers thought I'd like to see them Episcopals," she remarked regretfully. "Ef church air wa'n't so bad fer my rheumatiz, I'd pay car-fare jest to see it onct. I was brung up Methodist though."

This desire suggested to Amarilly's fertile little brain a way to make a contribution to John Meredith's pet missionary scheme, whose merits he had so ardently expounded from the pulpit.

"I'll hev a sacrud concert like the one he said they was goin' to hev to the church," she decided.

She was fully aware of the sensation created by the Thursday clothes-line of surplices, and she resolved to profit thereby while the garments were still a novelty. Consequently the neighborhood was notified that a sacred concert by a "surplused choir" composed of members of the Jenkins household, assisted by a few of their schoolmates, would be given a week from Wednesday night. This particular night was chosen for the reason that the church washing was put to soak late on a Wednesday.

There was a short, sharp conflict in Amarilly's conscience before she convinced herself it would not be wrong to allow the impromptu choir to don the surplices of St. Mark's.

"They wouldn't spile 'em jest awearin' 'em onct," she argued sharply, for Amarilly always "sassed back" with spirit to her moral accuser. "'Tain't as if they wa'n't agoin' into the wash as soon as they take 'em off. Besides," as a triumphant clincher, "think of the cause!"

Amarilly had heard the Boarder and a young socialist exchanging views, and she had caught this slogan, which was a tempting phrase and adequate to whitewash many a doubtful act. It proved effectual in silencing the conscience which Amarilly slipped back into its case and fastened securely.

She held nightly rehearsals for the proposed entertainment. After the first the novelty was exhausted, and on the next night there was a falling off in attendance, so the young, director diplomatically resorted to the use of decoy ducks in the shape of a pan of popcorn, a candy pull, and an apple roast. By such inducements she whipped her chorus into line, ably assisted by Bud, who had profited by his attendance at St. Mark's.

The Jenkins dwelling was singularly well adapted for a public performance, as, to use Mrs. Wint's phraseology, "it had no insides." The rooms were partitioned off by means of curtains on strings. These were taken down on the night of the concert. So the "settin'-room," the "bedroom off" and the kitchen became one. Seats were improvised by means of boards stretched across inverted washtubs.

At seven o'clock on the night set for the concert the audience was solemnly ushered in by the Boarder. No signs of the performers were visible, but sounds of suppressed excitement issued from the woodshed, which had been converted into a vestry.

Presently the choir, chanting a hymn, made an impressive and effective entrance. To Amarilly's consternation this evoked an applause, which jarred on her sense of propriety.

"This ain't no show, and it ain't no time to clap," she explained to the Boarder, who cautioned the congregation against further demonstration.

Flamingus read a psalm in a sing-song, resonant voice, and then Amarilly announced a hymn, cordially inviting the neighbors to "jine in." The response was lusty-lunged, and there was a unanimous request for another tune. After Amarilly had explained the use to which the collection was to be put, Gus passed a pie tin, while an offertory solo was rendered by Bud in sweet, trebled tones.

The sacred concert was pronounced a great success by the audience, who promptly dispersed at its close. While the Boarder was shifting the curtains to their former positions, and Mrs. Jenkins and Amarilly were busily engaged in divesting the choir of their costumes, the front door opened and disclosed a vision of loveliness in the form of Colette.

"I knocked," she explained apologetically to the Boarder, "but no one heard me. Are the family all away?"

"They are in the woodshed. Walk right out," he urged hospitably.

Colette stepped to the door and, on opening it, gazed in bewilderment at the disrobing choir.

"These are not St. Mark's choir-boys, are they?" she asked wonderingly.

Mrs. Jenkins felt herself growing weak-kneed. She looked apprehensively at Amarilly, who stepped bravely to the front with the air of one who feels that the end justifies the means.

"It was fer him—fer Mr. St. John I done it," she began in explanation, and then she proceeded to relate the particulars of her scheme and its accomplishment.

She had but just finished this narrative when suddenly in the line of her vision came the form of the young rector himself. He had been ushered out by the Boarder, who was still actively engaged in "redding up."

"I came to call upon you, for I consider you one of my parishioners now," he said to Amarilly, his face flushing at the unexpected encounter with Colette.

Amarilly breathed a devout prayer of thankfulness that the last surplice had been removed and was now being put to soak by her mother.

Colette's eyes were dancing with the delight of mischief-making as she directed, in soft but mirthful tones:

"Tell Mr. St. John about your choir and concert."

Amarilly's eyes lowered in consternation. She was in great awe of this young man whose square chin was in such extreme contradiction to his softly luminous eyes, and she began to feel less fortified by the reminder of the "cause."

"I'd ruther not," she faltered.

"Then don't, Amarilly," he said gently.

"Mebby that's why I'd orter," she acknowledged, lifting serious eyes to his. "You said that Sunday that we wa'n't to turn out of the way fer hard things."

"I don't want it to be hard for you to tell me anything, Amarilly," he said reassuringly. "Suppose you show me that you trust me by telling me about your concert."

So once more Amarilly gave a recital of her plan for raising money for the mission, and of its successful fulfilment. John listened with varying emotions, struggling heroically to maintain his gravity as he heard of the realization of the long-cherished, long-deferred dream of Mrs. Hudgers.

"And we took in thirty-seven cents," she said in breathless excitement, as she handed him the contents of the pie tin.

"Amarilly," he replied fervently, with the look that Colette was learning to love, "you did just right to use the surplices, and this contribution means more to me than any I have received. It was a sweet and generous thought that prompted your concert."

Amarilly's little heart glowed with pride at this acknowledgment.

At that moment came Bud, singing a snatch of his solo.

"Is this the little brother that sang the offertory?"

"Yes; that's him—Bud."

"Bud, will you sing it again for me, now?"

"Sure thing!" said the atom of a boy, promptly mounting a soap box.

He threw back a mop of thick black hair, rolled his eyes ceilingward, and let his sweet, clear voice have full sway.

"Oh, Bud, you darling! Why didn't you tell me he could sing like that,

Amarilly?" cried Colette at the close of the song.

"We must have him in St. Mark's choir," declared Mr. Meredith. "You may bring him to the rectory to-morrow, Amarilly, and I will have the choirmaster try his voice. Besides receiving instruction and practice every week, he will be paid for his singing."

Money for Bud's voice! So much prosperity was scarcely believable.

"Fust the Guild school, Miss King's washing, the surpluses, and now Bud!" thought Amarilly exuberantly. "Next thing I know, I'll be on the stage."

"I must go," said Colette presently. "My car is just around the corner on the next street. John, will you ride uptown with me?"

He accepted the invitation with alacrity. Colette's sidelong glance noted a certain masterful look about his chin, and there was a warning, metallic ring in his voice that denoted a determination to overcome all obstacles and triumph by sheer force of will. She was not ready to listen to him yet, and, a ready evader of issues, chatted incessantly on the way to the car. He waited in grim patience, biding his time. As they neared the turn in the alley, she played her reserve card.

"Henry didn't think it prudent to bring the big car into the Jenkins's cul-de-sac, so he waited in the next street. I expect father will be there by this time. We dropped him at a factory near by, where he was to speak to some United Workmen."

Colette smiled at the drooping of John's features as he beheld her father ensconced in the tonneau.

"Oh, John! I am glad you were here to protect my little girl through these byways. I was just on the point of looking her up myself."

When the car stopped at the rectory and Colette bade John good-night, the resolute, forward thrust was still prominent in his chin.

He went straight to his study and wrote an ardent avowal of his love. Then he sealed the letter and dispatched it by special messenger. There would be no more suspense, he thought, for she would have to respond by a direct affirmation or negation.

CHAPTER VII

In the tide of the Jenkins's prosperity there came the inevitable ebb. On the fateful Friday morning succeeding the concert, Mrs. Hudgers, looking from her window, saw a little group of children with books under their arms returning from school. Having no timepiece, she was accustomed to depend on the passing to and fro of the children for guidance as to the performance of her household affairs.

"My sakes, but twelve o'clock come quick to-day," she thought, as she kindled the fire and set the kettle over it in preparation of her midday meal.

A neighbor dropping in viewed these proceedings with surprise.

"Why, Mrs. Hudgers, ain't you et yer breakfast yet?"

"Of course I hev. I'm puttin' the kittle over fer my dinner."

"Dinner! why, it's only a half arter nine."

Mrs. Hudgers looked incredulous.

"I seen the chillern agoin' hum from school," she maintained.

"Them was the Jenkinses, Iry hez come down with the scarlit fever, and they're all in quarrytine."

"How you talk! Wait till I put the kittle offen the bile."

The two neighbors sat down to discuss this affliction with the ready sympathy of the poor for the poor. Their passing envy of the Jenkins's good fortune was instantly skimmed from the surface of their friendliness, which had only lain dormant and wanted but the touch of trouble to make them once more akin.

When the city physician had pronounced Iry's "spell" to be scarlet fever, the other members of the household were immediately summoned by emergency calls. The children came from school, Amarilly from the theatre, and the Boarder from his switch to hold an excited family conference.

"It's a good thing we got the washin's all hum afore Iry was took," declared the optimistic Amarilly.

"Thar's two things here yet," reported Mrs. Jenkins. "Gus come hum too late last night to take the preacher's surplus and Miss King's lace waist. You was so tired I didn't tell you, 'cause I know'd you'd be sot on goin' with them yourself. They're all did up."

"Well, they'll hev to stay right here with us and the fever," said

Amarilly philosophically.

At heart she secretly rejoiced in the retaining of these two garments, for they seemed to keep her in touch with their owners whom she would be unable to see until Iry had recovered.

"I don't see what we are going to do, Amarilly," said her mother despairingly. "Thar'll be nuthin' comin' in and so many extrys."

"No extrys," cheerfully assured the little comforter. "The city doctor'll take keer of Iry and bring the medicines. We hev laid by some sence we got the church wash. It'll tide us over till Iry gits well. We all need a vacation from work, anyhow."

At the beginning of the next week a ten-dollar bill came from Colette, "to buy jellies and things for Iry," she wrote. A similar contribution came from John Meredith.

"We air on Easy Street onct more!" cried Amarilly joyfully.

"I hate to take the money from them," sighed Mrs. Jenkins.

"We'll make it up to them when we kin work agin," consoled Amarilly.

"Better to take from friends than from the city. It won't be fer long.

Iry seems to hev took it light, the doctor said."

This diagnosis proved correct, but it had not occurred to Amarilly in her prognostications that the question of the duration of the quarantine was not entirely dependent upon Iry's convalescence. Like a row of blocks the children, with the exception of Flamingus and Amarilly, in rapid succession came down with a mild form of the fever. Mrs. Jenkins and Amarilly divided the labors of cook and nurse, but the mainstay of the family was the Boarder. He aided in the housework, and as an entertainer of the sick he proved invaluable. He told stories, drew pictures, propounded riddles, whittled boats and animals, played "Beggar my Neighbor," and sang songs for the convalescent ward.

When the last cent of the Jenkins's reserve fund and the contributions from the rector and Colette had been exhausted, the Boarder put a willing hand in his pocket and drew forth his all to share with the afflicted family. There was one appalling night when the treasury was entirely depleted, and the larder was a veritable Mother Hubbard's cupboard.

"Something will come," prophesied Amarilly trustfully.

Something did come the next day in the shape of a donation of five dollars from Mr. Vedder, who had heard of the prolonged quarantine. Amarilly wept from gratitude and gladness.

"The perfesshun allers stand by each other," she murmured proudly.

This last act of charity kept the Jenkins's pot boiling until the premises were officially and thoroughly fumigated. Again famine threatened. The switch remained open to the Boarder, and he was once more on duty, but he had as yet drawn no wages, one morning there was nothing for breakfast.

"I'll pawn my ticker at noon," promised the Boarder, "and bring home something for dinner."

"There is lots of folks as goes without breakfast allers, from choice," informed Amarilly. "Miss Vail, the teacher at the Guild, says it's hygeniack."

"It won't hurt us and the boys," said Mrs. Jenkins, "but Iry and Co is too young to go hungry even if it be hygeniack."

"They ain't agoin' hungry," declared Amarilly. "I'll pervide fer them."

With a small pitcher under her cape she started bravely forth on a foraging expedition. After walking a few blocks she came to a white house whose woodhouse joined the alley. Hiding behind a barrel she watched and waited until a woman opened the back door and set a soup plate of milk on the lowest step.

"Come a kits! Come a kits!" she called shrilly, and then went back into the house.

The "kits" came on the run; so did Amarilly. She arrived first, and hastily emptied the contents of the soup plate into her pitcher. Then she fled, leaving two dismayed maltese kittens disconsolately lapping an empty dish.

"Here's milk for Iry," she announced, handing the pitcher to her mother.

"Now I'll go and get some breakfast for Co."

She returned presently with a sugared doughnut.

"Where did you borry the milk and nut-cake?" asked her mother wonderingly.

"I didn't borry them," replied Amarilly stoically. "I stole them."

"Stole them! Am-a-ril-ly Jenk-ins!"

"Twan't exackly stealin'," argued Amarilly cheerfully. "I took the milk from two little cats what git stuffed with milk every morning and night. The doughnut had jest been stuck in a parrot's cage. He hedn't tetched it. My! he swore fierce! I'd ruther steal, anyway, than let Iry and Co go hungry."

"What would the preacher say!" demanded her mother solemnly. "He would say it was wrong."

"He don't know nothin' about bein' hungry!" replied Amarilly defiantly.

"If he was ever as hungry as Iry, I bet he'd steal from a cat."

The season was now summer. Some time ago John Meredith had gone to the seashore and the King family to their summer home in the mountains, unaware that the fever had spread over so wide an area in the Jenkins domain. The theatre and St. Mark's were closed for the rest of the summer. The little boys found that their positions had been filled during the period of quarantine. None of these catastrophes, however, could be compared to the calamity of the realization that Bud alone of all the patients had not convalesced completely. He was a delicate little fellow, and he grew paler and thinner each day. In desperation Amarilly went to the doctor.

"Bud don't pick up," she said bluntly.

"I feared he wouldn't," replied the doctor.

"Can't you try some other kinds of medicines?"

"I can, but I am afraid that there is no medicine that will help him very much."

Amarilly turned pale.

"Is there anything else that will help him?" she demanded fiercely.

"If he could go to the seashore he might brace up. Sea air would work wonders for him."

"He shall go," said Amarilly with determination.

"I can get a week for him through the Fresh Air Fund," suggested the doctor.

He succeeded in getting two weeks, and, that time was extended another fortnight through the benevolence of Mr. Vedder.

Bud returned a study in reds and browns.

"The sea beats the theayter and the church all to smitherines,

Amarilly!" he declared jubilantly. "I kin go to work now."

"No!" said Amarilly resolutely. "You air goin' to loaf through this hot weather until church and school open."

The family fund once more had a modest start. Mrs. Jenkins obtained a few of her old customers, Bobby got a paper route, Flamingus and Milton were again at work, but Amarilly, Gus, and Cory were without vocations.

Soon after the quarantine was lifted Amarilly went forth to deliver the surplice and the waist which had hung familiarly side by side during the weeks of trouble. The housekeeper at the rectory greeted her kindly and was most sympathetic on learning of the protracted confinement. She made Amarilly a present of the surplice.

"Mr. Meredith said you were to keep it. He thought your mother might find it useful. It is good linen, you know, and you can cut it up into clothes for the children. He has so many surplices, he won't miss this one."

"I'll never cut it up!" thought Amarilly as she reverently received the robe. "I'll keep it in 'membrance of him."

"It's orful good in him to give it to us," she said gratefully to the housekeeper.

That worthy woman smiled, remembering how the fastidious young rector had shrunk from the thought of wearing a fumigated garment.

At the King residence Amarilly saw the caretaker, who gave her a similar message regarding the lace waist.

"I'll keep it," thought Amarilly with a shy little blush, "until I'm married. It'll start my trousseau."

She took the garments home, not mentioning to anyone the gift of the waist, however, for that was to be her secret—her first secret. She hid this nest-egg of her trousseau in an old trunk which she fastened securely.

On the next day she was summoned to help clean the theatre, which had been rented for one night by the St. Andrew's vested choir, whose members were to give a sacred concert. A rehearsal for this entertainment was being held when Amarilly arrived.

"These surplices are all too long or too short for me," complained the young tenor, who had recently been engaged for the solo parts.

Amarilly surveyed him critically.

"He's jest about Mr. St. John's size," she mused, "only he ain't so fine a shape."

With the thought came an inspiration that brought a quickly waged battle. It seemed sacrilegious, although she didn't express it by that word, to permit another to wear a garment so sacred to the memory of Mr. Meredith, but poverty, that kill-sentiment, had fully developed the practical side of Amarilly.

She made answer to her stabs of conscience by action instead of words, going straight to her friend, the ticket-seller.

"That feller," she said, indicating the tenor, "ain't satisfied with the fit of his surplus. I've got one jest his size. It's done up spick and span clean, and I'll rent it to him fer the show. He kin hev it fer the ev'nin' fer a dollar. Would you ask him fer me?"

"Certainly, Amarilly," he agreed.

He came back to her, smiling.

"He'll take it, but he seems to think your charge rather high — more than that of most costumers, he said."

"This ain't no common surplus," defended Amarilly loftily. "It was wore by the rector of St. Mark's, and he give it to me. It's of finer stuff than the choir surpluses, and it hez got a cross worked onto it, and a pocket in it, too."

"Of course such inducements should increase the value," confirmed Mr. Vedder gravely, and he proceeded to hold another colloquy with the twinkling-eyed tenor. Amarilly went home for the surplice and received therefor the sum of one dollar, which swelled the Jenkins's purse perceptibly.

And here began the mundane career of the minister's surplice.

CHAPTER VIII

Ever apt in following a lead, Amarilly at once resolved to establish a regular costuming business. It even occurred to her to hire out the lace waist, but thoughts of wedding bells prevailed against her impulse to open this branch of the business.

When the young tenor returned the surplice he informed Amarilly that two young ladies of his acquaintance were going to give a home entertainment for charity. Among the impromptu acts would be some tableaux, and the surplice was needed for a church scene. So the new venture brought in another dollar that week.

One day Bud came home capless, having crossed a bridge in a high wind.

"I seen an ad," said the thrifty Flamingus, "that the Beehive would give away baseball caps to-day."

Amarilly immediately set out for the Beehive, an emporium of fashion in the vicinity of the theatre. It was the noon hour, and there were no other customers in evidence.

The proprietor and a clerk were engaged in discussing the design for a window display, and were loath to notice their would-be beneficiary. Finally the clerk drawled out:

"Did you want anything, little girl?"

"I called," explained Amarilly with grandiose manner, "to git one of them caps you advertised to give away."

"Oh, those were all given out long ago. You should have come earlier," he replied with an air of relief, as he turned to resume the all-absorbing topic with the proprietor.

Amarilly's interest in the window display dispelled any disappointment she might have had in regard to Bud's head covering.

"Now," said the clerk didactically, "my idea is this. Have a wedding—a church wedding. I can rig up an altar, and we'll have the bride in a white, trailing gown; the groom, best man, and ushers in dress suits to advertise our gents' department, the bridesmaids and relatives in different colored evening dresses, and in this way we can announce our big clearing sale of summer goods in the ready-to-wear department. It'll make a swell window and draw crowds. Women can never get by a wedding."

"That's a dandy idea, Ben," approved the proprietor.

"Oh, I am a winner on ideas," vaunted the clerk chestily.

So was Amarilly. She stepped eagerly up to the window designer.

"Do you keep surpluses?"

"No; don't know what they are," replied the clerk shortly, turning from her. "We'll get a wreath of orange flowers for the bride, and then we can have a child carrying the ring, so as to call attention to our children's department."

"A surplus," explained Amarilly, scornful of such avowed ignorance, "is the white gown that Episcopal ministers wear."

"No; we don't keep them," was the impatient rejoinder.

"Well, I hev one," she said, addressing the proprietor this time, "a real minister's, and I'll rent it to you to put on your figger of the minister in your wedding window. He'll hev to wear one."

"I am not an Episcopalian," said the proprietor hesitatingly. "What do you think, Ben?"

"Well, it hadn't occurred to me to have an Episcopal wedding, but I don't know but what it would work out well, after all. It would make it attract notice more, and women are always daffy over Episcopal weddings. They like classy things. We could put a card in the window, saying all the clergy bought the linen for their surplices here. How," turning to Amarilly, "did you happen to have such an article?"

"We do the washin' fer St. Mark's church, and the minister give us one of his surpluses."

"The display will be in for six days. What will you rent it for that long?"

"I allers git a dollar a night fer it," replied Amarilly.

"Too much!" declared the clerk. "I'll give you fifty cents a day."

"I'll let it go six days fer four dollars," bargained Amarilly.

"Well, seeing you have come down on your offer, I'll come up a little on mine. I'll take it for three-fifty."

Amarilly considered.

"I will, if you'll throw in one of them caps fer my brother."

"All right," laughed the proprietor. "I think we'll call it a bargain. See if you can't dig up one of those caps for her, Ben."

Without much difficulty Ben produced a cap, and Amarilly hurried home for the surplice. She went down to the Beehive every day during the wedding-window week and feasted her eyes on the beloved gown. She took all the glory of the success of the display to her own credit, and her feelings were very much like those of the writer of a play on a first night.

From a wedding to a funeral was the natural evolution of a surplice, but this time it did not appear in its customary rôle. Instead of adorning a minister, it clad the corpse. Mrs. Hudgers's only son, a scalawag, who had been a constant drain on his mother's small stipend, was taken ill and died, to the discreetly disguised relief of the neighborhood.

"I'm agoin' to give Hallie a good funeral," Mrs. Hudgers confided to

Amarilly. "I'm agoin' to hev hacks and flowers and singin' If yer St.

Mark's man was to hum now, I should like to have him fishyate."

"Who will you git?" asked Amarilly interestedly.

"I'll hev the preacher from the meetin'-house on the hill, Brother

Longgrass."

"I wonder," speculated Amarilly, "if he'd like to wear the surplus?"

Foremost as the plumes of Henry of Navarre in battle were the surplice and the renting thereof in Amarilly's vision.

"I don't expect he could do that," replied Mrs. Hudgers doubtfully. "His church most likely wouldn't stand fer it. Brother Longgrass is real kind if he ain't my sort. He's agoin' to let the boys run the maylodeun down here the night afore the funyral."

"Who's agoin' to sing?"

"I dunno yit. I left it to the preacher. He said he'd git me a picked choir, whatever that may be."

"My! But you'll hev a fine funeral!" exclaimed Amarilly admiringly.

"I allers did say that when Hallie got married, or died, things should be done right. Thar's jest one thing I can't hev."

"What's that, Mrs. Hudgers?"

"Why, you see, Amarilly, Hallie's clo'es air sort of shabby-like, and when we git him in that shiny new caskit, they air agoin' to show up orful seedy. But I can't afford ter buy him a new suit jest for this onct."

"Couldn't you rent a suit?" asked Amarilly, her ruling passion for business still dominating.

"No; I jest can't, Amarilly. It's costin' me too much now."

"I know it is," sympathized Amarilly, concentrating her mind on the puzzling solution of Hallie's habiliment.

"Mrs. Hudgers," she exclaimed suddenly, "why can't you put the surplus on Hallie? You kin slip it on over his suit, and when the funeral's over, and they hev all looked at the corpse, you kin take it offen him."

"Oh, that would be sweet!" cried Mrs. Hudgers, brightening perceptibly. "Hallie would look beautiful in it, and 'twould be diffrent from any one else's funeral. How you allers think of things, Amarilly! But I ain't got no dollar to pay you fer it."

"If you did hev one," replied Amarilly Indignantly, "I shouldn't let you pay fer it. We're neighbors, and what I kin do fer Hallie I want ter do."

"Well, Amarilly, it's certainly fine fer you to feel that way. You don't think," she added with sudden apprehension, "that they'd think the surplus was Hallie's nightshirt, do you?"

"Oh, no!" protested Amarilly, shocked at such a supposition. "Besides, you kin tell them all that Hallie's laid out in a surplus. They all seen them to the concert."

The funeral passed off with great éclat. The picked choir had resonant voices, and Brother Longgrass preached one of his longest sermons, considerably omitting reference to any of the characteristics of the deceased. Mrs. Hudgers was suitably attired in donated and dusty black. The extremely unconventional garb of Hallie caused some little comment, but it was commonly supposed to be a part of the Episcopalian spirit which the Jenkinses seemed to be inculcating in the neighborhood. Brother Longgrass was a little startled upon beholding the white-robed corpse, but perceiving what comfort it brought to the afflicted mother, he magnanimously forbore to allude to the matter.

After the remains had been viewed for the last time, the surplice was removed. In the evening Amarilly called for it.

"He did look handsome in it," commented Mrs. Hudgers with a satisfied, reminiscent smile. "I wish I might of hed his likeness took. I'm agoin' to make you take hum this pan of fried cakes Mrs. Holdock fetched in. They'll help fill up the chillern."

"I don't want to rob you, Mrs. Hudgers," said Amarilly, gazing longingly at the doughnuts, which were classed as luxuries in the Jenkins's menu.

"I dassent eat 'em, Amarilly. If I et jest one, I'd hev dyspepsy orful, and folks hez brung in enough stuff to kill me now. It does beat all the way they bring vittles to a house of mournin'! I only wish Hallie could hev some of 'em."

CHAPTER IX

The surplice, carefully laundered after the funeral, was ready for new fields of labor. The tenor, first patron of Amarilly's costuming establishment, was wont to loiter in the studio of an artist he knew and relate his about-town adventures. This artist was interested in the annals of the little scrub-girl and her means of livelihood.

"I have in mind," he said musingly, "a picture of a musician, the light to be streaming through a stained window on his uplifted head as he sits at an organ."

"The Lost Chord?" inquired the tenor.

"Nothing quite so bromidic as that," laughed the artist. "I have my model engaged, and I had intended to have you borrow a surplice for me, but you may ask your little customer to rent me her gown for a couple of days."

On receipt of this request delivered through the medium of the ticket-seller, Amarilly promptly appeared at the studio. She was gravely and courteously received by the artist, Derry Phillips, an easy-mannered youth, slim and supple, with dark, laughing eyes. When they had transacted the business pertaining to the rental of the surplice, Amarilly arose from her chair with apparent reluctance. This was a new atmosphere, and she was fascinated by the pictures and the general air of artistic disarrangement which she felt but could not account for.

"'Tain't exactly the kind of place to tidy," she reflected, "but it needs cleaning turrible."

"Do you like pictures?" asked the young artist, following her gaze.

"Stay a while and look at them, if you wish."

Amarilly readily availed herself of this permission, and rummaged about the rooms while Derry pursued his work. Upon the completion of her tour of inspection, he noticed a decided look of disapproval upon her face.

"What is the matter, Miss Jenkins? Aren't the pictures true to life?" he inquired with feigned anxiety.

"The picters is all right," replied Amarilly, "but—"

"But what?" he urged expectantly.

"Your rooms need reddin' up. Thar's an orful lot of dust. Yer things will spile."

"Oh, dust, you know, to the artistic temperament, is merely a little misplaced matter."

"'Tain't only misplaced. It's stuck tight," contended Amarilly.

"Dear me! And to think that I was contemplating a studio tea to some people day after to-morrow, I suppose it really should be 'red up' again. Honestly though, I engage a woman who come every week and clean the rooms."

"She's imposed on you," said Amarilly indignantly. "She's swept the dirt up agin the mopboards and left it thar, and she hez only jest skimmed over things with a dust-cloth. It ain't done thorough."

"And are you quite proficient as a blanchisseuse?"

Amarilly looked at him unperturbed.

"I kin scrub," she remarked calmly.

"I stand rebuked. Scrubbing is what they need. If you will come to-morrow morning and put these rooms in order, I will give you a dollar and your midday meal."

Amarilly, well satisfied with her new opening, closed the bargain instantly.

The next morning at seven o'clock she rang the studio bell. The artist, attired in a bathrobe and rubbing his eyes sleepily, opened the door.

"This was the day I was to clean," reminded Amarilly reprovingly.

"To be sure. But why so early? I thought you were a telegram."

"Early! It's seven o'clock."

"I still claim it's early. I have only been in bed four hours."

"Well, you kin go back to bed. I'll work orful quiet."

"And I can trust you not to touch any of the pictures or move anything?"

"I'll be keerful," Amarilly assured him. "Jest show me whar to het up the water. I brung the soap and a brush."

The artist lighted a gas stove, and, after carefully donning a long- sleeved apron, Amarilly put the water on and began operations. Her eyes shone with anticipation as she looked about her.

"I'm glad it's so dirty," she remarked. "It's more interestin' to clean a dirty place. Then what you do shows up, and you feel you earnt your money."

With a laugh the artist returned to his bedroom, whence he emerged three hours later.

"This room is all cleaned," announced Amarilly. "It took me so long 'cause it's so orful big and then 'twas so turrible dirty."

"You must have worked like a little Trojan. Now stop a bit while I prepare my breakfast."

"Kin you cook?" asked Amarilly in astonishment.

"I can make coffee and poach eggs. Come into my butler's pantry and watch me."

Amarilly followed him into a small apartment and was initiated into the mysteries of electric toasters and percolators.

He tried in vain to induce her to share his meal with him, but she protested.

"I hed my breakfast at five-thirty. I don't eat agin till noon."

"Oh, Miss Jenkins! You have no artistic temperament or you would not cling to ironclad rules."

"My name's Amarilly," she answered shortly. "I ain't old enough to be 'missed' yet."

"I beg your pardon, Amarilly. You seem any age," he replied, sitting down to his breakfast, "You are not too old, then, for me to ask what your age is — in years?"

"I jest got into my teens."

"Thirteen. And I am ten years older. When is your birthday?"

"It's ben. It was the fust of June."

"Why, Amarilly," jumping up and holding out his hand, "we are twins! That is my birthday."

"And you are twenty-three."

"Right you are. That is my age at the present moment. Last night I was far older, and to-morrow, mayhap, I'll be years younger."

"Be you a Christian Science?" she asked doubtfully.

"Lord, no, child! I am an artist. What made you ask that?"

"'Cause they don't believe in age. Miss Jupperskin told me about 'em. She's workin' up to it. But I must go back to my work."

"So must I, Amarilly. My model will be here in a few moments to don your surplice. If you want to clean up my breakfast dishes you may do so, and then tackle the bedroom and the rest of the apartment."

Three hours later, Amarilly went into the studio. The model had gone, and the artist stood before his easel surveying his sketch with approval.

"This is going to be a good picture, Amarilly. The model caught my idea. There is some fore—"

"Mr. Phillips!"

"My name is Derry. I am too young to be 'mistered.'"

There was no response, and with a smile he turned inquiringly toward her. There was a wan little droop about the corners of her eyes and lips that brought contrition to his boyish heart.

"Amarilly you are tired! You have worked too steadily. Sit down and rest awhile."

"'Tain't that! I'm hungry. Kin I het up the coffee and—"

"Good gracious, Amarilly! I forgot you ate at regular, stated intervals. We will go right out now to a nice little restaurant near by and eat our luncheon together."

Amarilly flushed.

"Thank you, Mr. Derry. That's orful nice in you, but I'd ruther eat here. Thar's the toast and coffee to het, and an aig—"

"No! You are going to have a good, square meal and eat it with me. You see I had to eat my birthday dinner all alone, so we'll celebrate the first of June now, together. Slip off your apron. By the way, some day I shall paint a picture of you in that apron scrubbing my 'mopboard.'"

Amarilly shook her head.

"I don't look fit to go nowhars with you, Mr. Derry."

"Vanitas, and the rest of it! Oh, Amarilly, only thirteen, and the ruling passion of your sex already in full sway!"

"It's on your account that I'm ashamed," she said in defence of his accusation. "I'd want ter look nice fer you."

"That's sweet of you, Amarilly; but if you really want to look nice, don't think of your clothes. It's other things. Think of your hair, for instance. It's your best point, and yet you hide it under a bushel and, worse than that, you braid it so tight I verily believe it's wired."

"I'm used to bein' teased about my red head," she replied. "I don't keer."

"It's a glorious red, Amarilly. The color the vulgar jeer at, and artists like your friend and twin, Derry, rave over. You're what is called 'Titian-haired,'"

"Are you makin' fun, Mr. Derry?" she asked suspiciously.

"No, Amarilly; seriously, I think it the loveliest shade of hair there is, and now I am going to show you how you should wear it. Unbind it, all four of those skin-tight braids."

She obeyed him, and a loosened, thick mass of hair fell below her waist.

"Glorious!" he cried fervidly. "Take that comb from the top of your head and comb it out. There! Now part it, and catch up these strands loosely — so. I must find a ribbon for a bow. What color would you suggest, Amarilly?"

"Brown."

"Bravo, Amarilly. If you had said blue, I should have lost all faith in your future upcoming. Here are two most beautiful brown bows on this thingamajig some one gave me last Christmas, and whose claim on creation I never discovered. Let me braid your hair loosely for two and one-quarter inches. One bow here — another there. Look in the glass, Amarilly. If I give you these bows will you promise me never to wear your hair in any other fashion until you are sixteen at least? Off with your apron! It's picturesque, but soapy and exceedingly wet. You won't need a hat. It's only around the corner, and I want your hair to be observed and admired."

Amarilly gained assurance from the reflection of her hair in the mirror, and they started gayly forth like two school children out for a lark. He ushered her into a quiet little café that had an air of pronounced elegance about it. In a secluded corner behind some palms came the subdued notes of stringed instruments. Derry seemed to be well known here, and his waiter viewed his approach with an air of proprietorship.

"It's dead quiet here," thought Amarilly wonderingly. "Like a church."

It was beginning to dawn upon her alert little brain that real things were all quiet, not noisy like the theatre.

"What shall we have first, Amarilly?" inquired her new friend with mock deference. "Bouillon?"

Amarilly, recalling the one time in her life when she had had "luncheon," replied casually that she preferred fruit, and suggested a melon.

"Good, Amarilly! You are a natural epicure. Fruit, certainly, on a warm day like this. I shall let you select all the courses. What next?"

"Lobster," she replied nonchalantly.

"Fine! And then?"

"Grapefruit salad."

He looked at her in amazement, and reflected that she had doubtless been employed in some capacity that had made her acquainted with luncheon menus.

"And," concluded Amarilly, without waiting for prompting, "I think an ice would be about right. And coffee in a little cup, and some cheese."

"By all means, Amarilly," he responded humbly. "And what kind of cheese, please?"

"Now I'm stumped," thought Amarilly ruefully, "fer I can't 'member how to speak the kind she hed."

"Most any kind," she said loftily, "except that kind you put in mousetraps."

"Oh, Amarilly, you are a true aristocrat! How comes it that you scrub floors? Is it on a bet?"

The waiter came up and said something to the artist in a low tone, and

Derry replied hastily:

"Nothing to-day." Then, turning to Amarilly, he asked her if she would like a glass of milk. Upon her assent, he ordered two glasses of milk, to the veiled surprise of the waiter.

When the luncheon was served, Amarilly, by reason of her good memory, was still at ease. The children at the Guild school had been given a few general rules in table deportment, but Amarilly had followed every movement of Colette's so faithfully at the eventful luncheon that she ate very slowly, used the proper forks and spoons, and won Derry's undisguised admiration.

"Mr. Vedder's, good," she thought. "Mr. St. John's grand, but this 'ere Mr. Derry's folksy. I'd be skeert settin' here eatin' with Mr. St. John, but this feller's only a kid, and I feel quite to hum with him."

"Amarilly," he said confidentially, as they were sipping their coffee from "little cups," "you are truthful, I know. Will you be perfectly frank with me and answer a question?"

"Mebby," she replied warily.

"Did you ever eat a luncheon like this before?"

"I never seen the inside of a restyrant afore," she replied.

"Now you are fencing. I mean, did you ever have the same things to eat that we had just now?"

Amarilly hesitated, longing to mystify him further, but it came over her in a rush how very kind he had been to her.

"Yes, I hev. I'll tell you all about it."

"Good! An after-dinner story! Beat her up, Amarilly!"

So she told him of her patroness and the luncheon she had eaten at her house.

"And I watched how she et and done, and she tole me the names of the things we hed. I writ them out, and that was my lesson that night with the Boarder."

Then, of course, Derry must know all about the Boarder and the brothers. After she had finished her faithful descriptions, it was time to return to the studio. Her quick, keen eyes had noted the size of the bill Derry had put on the salver, and the small amount of change he had received. She walked home beside him in troubled silence.

"What's the matter, Amarilly?" he asked as she was buttoning on her apron preparatory to resuming work. "Didn't the luncheon agree with you, or are you mad at me? And for why, pray?"

Amarilly's thin little face flushed and a tear came into each thoughtful eye.

"I hedn't orter to hev tole you ter git all them things. I was atryin' ter be smart and show off, but, honest, I didn't know they was agoin' ter cost so much. I ain't agoin' ter take no money fer the cleanin', and that'll help some."

Derry laughed rapturously.

"My dear child!" he exclaimed, when he could speak. "You are a veritable little field daisy. You really saved me money by going with me. If I had gone alone, I should have spent twice as much."

"How could that be?" she asked unbelievingly. "You would only hev give one order, so 'twould hev ben jest half as much."

"But if you had not been with me, I should have had a cocktail and a bottle of wine, which would have cost more than our meal. Out of deference to your youth and other things, I forbore to indulge. So you see I saved money by having you along. And then it was much better for me not to have had those libations."

"Honest true?"

"Honest true, hope to die! Cross my heart and all the rest of it! I'd lie cheerfully to some people, but never to you, Amarilly."

"My. Reeves-Eggleston — he's on the stage — said artists was allers poor."

"That's one reason why I am not an artist — a great artist. I am hampered by an inheritance that allows me to live without working, so I don't do anything worth while. I only dabble at this and that. Some day, maybe, I'll have an inspiration."

"Go to work now," she admonished.

"I must perforce. My model's foot is on the stair."

Amarilly left the studio to resume her cleaning. At five o'clock she came back. Derry stood at the window, working furiously at some fleecy clouds sailing over a cerulean sky. She was about to speak, but discerning that he must work speedily and uninterruptedly to keep pace with the shifting clouds, she refrained.

"There!" he said. "I got it. You were a good little girl not to interrupt me, Amarilly."

"It's beautiful!" gasped Amarilly. "I was afeard you'd git the sky blue instead of purplish and that you'd make the clouds too white."

"Amarilly, you've the soul of an artist! In you I have found a true critic."

"Come and see if the rooms is all right. I got 'em real clean. Every nook and corner. And—"

"I know you did, Amarilly, without looking. I can smell the clean from here."

"If thar's nothin' more you want did, I'll go hum."

"Here's a dollar for the rooms and two dollars for the surplice. Amarilly, you were glad to learn table manners from Miss King, weren't you?"

"Yes; I like to larn all I kin."

"Then, will you let me teach you something?"

"Sure!" she acquiesced quickly.

"There are two things you must do for me. Never say 'et'; say 'ate' instead. Then you must say 'can'; not 'kin.' It will be hard to remember at first, but every time you forget and make a mistake, remember to-day and our jolly little luncheon, will you?"

"I will, and I can, Mr. Derry."

"You're an apt little pupil, Amarilly, and I am going to teach you two words every time you come."

"Oh!" exclaimed Amarilly, brightening. "Will you want me ter come agin?"

"Indeed I shall. I am going away next week to the mountains for a couple of months. When I come back, I am going to have you come every morning at nine o'clock. You can prepare and serve my simple breakfast and clean my rooms every day. Then they won't get so disreputable. I will pay you what they do at the theatre, and it will not be such hard work. Will you enjoy it as well?"

"Oh, better!" exclaimed Amarilly.

And with this naive admission died the last spark of Amarilly's stage-lust.

"Then consider yourself engaged. You can call for the surplice to-morrow afternoon at this hour."

"Thank you, Mr. Derry."

She hesitated, and then awkwardly extended her hand, which he shook most cordially.

"Thank you for a day's entertainment, Amarilly. I haven't been bored once. You have very nice hands," looking down at the one he still held.

She reddened and jerked her hand quickly away.

"Now you are kiddin'! They're redder than my hair, and rough and big."

"I repeat, Amarilly, you have nice hands. It isn't size and color that counts; it's shape, and from an artist's standpoint you have shapely hands. Now will you be good, and shake hands with me in a perfectly ladylike way? Thank you, Amarilly."

"Thank you, Mr. Derry. It's the beautifulest day I ever hed. Better'n the matinée or the Guild or—" she drew a quick breath and said in a scared whisper—"the church!"

"I am flattered, Amarilly. We shall have many ruby-lettered days like it."

CHAPTER X

The next afternoon Amarilly called at the studio for the surplice.

"I am glad to see you have your hair fixed as I told you, Amarilly," was Derry's greeting. "And have you remembered the other things I told you?"

"I hev' writ out 'can' and 'ate' in big letters and pinned 'em up on the wall. I can say 'em right every time now."

"Of course you can! And for a reward here's a dollar with which to buy some black velvet hair-ribbons. Never put any color but black or brown near your hair, Amarilly."

"No, Mr. Derry; but I don't want to take the dollar."

"See here, Amarilly! You're to be my little housemaid, and the uniform is always provided. Instead of buying you a cap and apron, I prefer to furnish velvet hair-ribbons. Take it, and get a good quality silk velvet. And now, good-by for two months. I will let you know when I am home so that you may begin on your duties."

"Good-by, Mr. Derry," said the little girl artlessly. "And thar's something I'd like to say to you, if you don't mind."

"You may say anything—everything—to me, Amarilly."

"When you go to eat, won't you order jest as ef I was with you—nothin' more?"

His fair boyish face reddened slightly, and then a serious look came into his dancing eyes.

"By Jove, Amarilly! I've been wishing some girl who really meant it, who really cared, would say that to me. You put it very delicately and sweetly. I'll—yes, I'll do it all the time I'm gone. There's my hand on it. Good-by, Amarilly."

"Good-by, Mr. Derry."

Amarilly walked home very slowly, trying to think of a way to realize again from the surplice.

"I'm afeerd I won't find a place to rent it right away," she sighed.

Looking up, she saw the Boarder. A slender, shy slip of a girl had his arm, and he was gazing into her intent eyes with a look of adoration.

"Oh, the Boarder is in love!" gasped Amarilly; her responsive little heart leaping in sympathetic interest. "That's why he's wore a blue necktie the last few days. Lord Algernon said that was allers a sure sign."

She tactfully slipped around a corner, unseen by the entranced couple.

That night, as he was lighting his after-supper pipe, the Boarder remarked casually:

"I'd like to rent the surplus fer an hour to-morrer, Amarilly."

"Why, what on airth can you do with it?" was the astonished query.

The Boarder looked sheepish.

"You see, Amarilly, I'm akeepin' stiddy company with a little gal."

"I seen you and her this arternoon. She's orful purty," said Amarilly reflectively. "She looked kinder delikit, though. What's her name?"

"Lily — Lily Rose. Ain't that a purty name?"

"Beautiful. The lily part jest suits her. She's like a flower — a white flower. But what do you want the surplus fer?"

"You see," began the Boarder, coming by circuitous route to his subject, "gals git notions in their heads sometimes when they air in—"

"Love," promptly supplied the comprehending little girl.

"Yes," he assented with a fiery blush. "And she wants fer me to hev my likeness took so I kin give it to her."

"Thar ain't nothin' foolish about that!" declared Amarilly.

"No; but I never sot fer one yet. I wouldn't mind, but you see she's got it in her head that I am good-looking—"

"Well, you be," corroborated Amarilly decisively.

"And she wants me fer to dress up like a preacher. I told her about Hallie Hudgers lookin' so swell in the surplus, and she wants, as I should dress up in it and set fer my likeness in it."

"I think it would be fine!" approved Amarilly. "You sure would look nicer nor Hallie did."

"Well, I wouldn't look like a dead one," admitted the Boarder. "But I was orful afraid you'd laugh. Then I kin rent it fer an hour to-morrer ef it ain't got no other dates."

"You can't rent it. You can take it fer an hour, or so long as you like," she assured him.

"You'll hev to take a quarter anyway, fer luck. Mebby 'twill bring me luck awinnin' her."

The photograph of the Boarder in saintly attire was pronounced a great success. Before the presentation he had it set in a frame made of gilt network studded with shells.

Lily Rose spent her leisure moments gazing upon it with the dream-centred eyes of a young devotee before a shrine.

The next wearing of the surplice was more in accord with its original design. In the precinct adjoining the one in which lived and let live the Jenkins family, a colored Episcopal church had recently been established. The rector had but one surplice, and that had been stolen from the clothes-line, mayhap by one of his dusky flock; thus it was that Amarilly received a call from the Reverend Virgil Washington, who had heard of the errant surplice, which he offered to purchase.

Naturally his proposition was met by a firm and unalterable refusal. It would have been like selling a golden goose to dispose of such a profitable commodity. He then asked to rent it for a Sunday while he was having one made. This application, being quite in Amarilly's line of business, met with a ready assent.

"You can hev it fer a dollar," she offered.

The bargain was finally closed, although it gave Amarilly more than a passing pang to think of the snowy folds of Mr. St. John's garment adorning an Ethiopian form.

One day there came to the Jenkins home a most unusual caller. The novel presence of the "mailman" at their door brought every neighbor to post of observation. His call was for the purpose of leaving a gayly-colored postal card addressed to "Miss Amarilly Jenkins." It was from Derry, and she spent many happy moments in deciphering it. His writing was microscopic, and he managed to convey a great deal of information in the allotted small space. He inquired solicitously concerning the surplice, and bade her be a good girl and not forget the two words he had taught her. "I have ordered all my meals as though you were with me," he wrote in conclusion.

Amarilly laid the card away with her wedding waist. Then, with the

Boarder's aid, she indited an answer on a card that depicted the Barlow

Theatre.

The next event for Amarilly was an invitation to attend the wedding of Mrs. Hubbleston, a buxom, bustling widow for whom Mrs. Jenkins washed. In delivering the clothes, Amarilly had come to be on very friendly terms with the big, light-hearted woman, and so she had been asked to assist in the serving of refreshments on the eventful night.

"I've never been to a wedding," said Amarilly wistfully. "I've been to most everything else, and I would like to see you wed, but I ain't got no clo'es 'cept my hair-ribbons."

Mrs. Hubbleston looked at her contemplatively.

"My last husband's niece's little girl left a dress here once when she was going home after a visit. She had hardly worn it, but she had outgrown it, and her ma told me to give it away. I had 'most forgotten about it. I believe it would just fit you. Let us see."

She produced a white dress that adjusted itself comfortably to

Amarilly's form.

"You look real pretty in white, Amarilly. You shall have this dress for your own."

On the nuptial night Amarilly, clad in the white gown and with black velvet hair-ribbons, went forth at an early hour to the house of festivity.

Mrs. Hubbleston, resplendent in a glittering jetted gown, came into the kitchen to see that things were progressing properly.

"Ain't you flustered?" asked Amarilly, looking at her in awe.

"Land, no, child! I have been married four times before this, you see, so it comes natural. There goes the doorbell. It must be Mr. Jimmels and the minister."

In a few moments she returned to the kitchen for sympathy.

"I am so disappointed," she sighed, "but then, I might have expected something would happen. It always does at my weddings."

"What is it?" asked Amarilly, apprehensive lest the wedding might be declared off.

"I've been married once by a Baptist minister, once by a Methodist, and the third time by a Congregationalist; last time a Unitarian tied the knot. So this once I thought I would have an Episcopal, because their white robe lends tone. And Rev. Mr. Woodthorn has come without his. He says he never brings it to the house weddings unless specially requested. He lives clear across the city, and the carriage has gone away."

"Oh, I have a surplus!" cried Amarilly enthusiastically. "I'll telephone our grocer. Milt's ahelpin' him to-night, and he can ride over here on the grocer's wheel and fetch it."

"Why, how in the world did you come by such a thing as a surplice?" asked the widow in surprise.

Amarilly quickly explained, and then telephoned to her brother.

"He says he'll be over here in a jiffy," she announced. "And ain't it lucky, it's jest been did up clean!"

"My, but that's fortunate! It'll be the making of my wedding. I shall give you a dollar for the use of it, the same as those others did."

"No!" objected Amarilly. "Ill be more than glad to let you hev it arter your givin' me this fine dress."

"I'll have Mr. Jimmels pay you for it. He can take a dollar out of the fee for the minister. It will serve him right for not bringing all his trappings with him."

Amarilly's sense of justice was appeased by this arrangement. She went into the double parlors to witness the ceremony, which gave her a few little heart thrills.

"Them words sounds orful nice," she thought approvingly. "The Boarder and Lily Rose must hev an Episcopal fer to marry them. I wonder if I'll ever get to Miss King's and Mr. St. John's weddin' or Mr. Derry's; but I guess he'll never be married. He jokes too much to be thinkin' of sech things." Then came the thought of her own wedding garment awaiting its destiny.

"I ain't even hed a beau, yet," she sighed, "but the Boarder says that I will— that red-headed girls ain't never old maids from ch'ice."

With this sustaining thought, she proceeded to the dining-room. She had been taught at the Guild how to wait on table, and she proved herself to be very deft and capable in putting her instructions into effect.

"Here's two dollars," the complacent bride said to Amarilly before departing. "One is for serving so nicely, and one is for the surplice. I told them in the kitchen to put you up a basket of things to take home to the children."

Amarilly thanked her profusely and then went home. She deposited her two dollars in the family exchequer, and proceeded to distribute the contents of the basket.

"Now, set around the table here, and take what I give you. Thar ain't enough of one thing to go hull way round, except fer ma. She's agoin' to hev some of each. Yes, you be, ma. This here baskit's mine. Here's a sandwich, some chicken, salid, jell, two kinds of cake, and some ice- cream fer you. Bud can hev first pick now, 'cause he ain't so strong as the rest of you. All right, Bud; take the rest of the ice-cream and some cake."

"'Tain't fair! I'm a girl, and I'm younger than Bud. I'd orter choose first," sobbed Cory.

"Shut up, Co! You'll wake Iry, and then he'll hev to hev something, and if he sleeps right through, thar'll be jest so much more fer you. 'Twon't hurt him to miss what he don't know about. All right, Cory, you can hev cake and jell. That's a good boy, Bud, to give her two tastes of the cream, and ma'll give you two more. Bobby? Sandwiches and pickle. Milt? Chicken and salid. Flammy and Gus, pickle and sandwich is all that's left fer you. The rest of this chicken is agoin' into the Boarder's dinner pail to-morrer."

CHAPTER XI

Milton came home from the grocery one night with a telephone message from Mr. Vedder requesting Amarilly to bring the surplice to his rooms on the next day.

"How is business?" asked the ticket-seller kindly, when the little girl appeared in answer to his summons.

"Fine! The surplus has brung in nine dollars and seventy-five cents a'ready. It's kept things goin'."

"The theatre will open in a couple of weeks, and then you will have steady work, though I wish we might get an easier and pleasanter occupation for you."

"I'm agoin' to hev one, Mr. Vedder," and she proceeded to tell him of

Derry and her engagement at his studio.

"It kinder seems as if I b'longed to the theayter, and you've been so orful kind to me, Mr. Vedder, that it'll seem strange-like not to be here, but Mr. Phillips's work'll be a snap fer me."

"You've been a good, faithful little girl, Amarilly, and I shall want to keep track of you and see you occasionally, so I am going to give you a pass to every Saturday matinée during the winter."

"Oh, Mr. Vedder, there's been no one so good as you've been to me! And you never laugh at me like other folks do."

"No, indeed, child! Why should I? But I never knew before that you had such beautiful hair!"

"It's 'cause it's fixed better," said Amarilly with a blush. "But who wants the surplus this time?"

"I do," he replied smiling. "I am invited to a sheet and pillow-case party. I thought this surplice would be more comfortable than a sheet. Here's a dollar for it."

"No," declined Amarilly firmly. "Not arter all you've done fer us. I won't take it."

"Amarilly," he said earnestly. "I have no one in the world to do anything for, and sometimes, when I get to thinking about it, I am very lonely. So if you want to be kind to me, you will give me the pleasure of helping you a little now and then. I shall not enjoy the party unless you will take the money."

Amarilly cried a little that night, thinking how good he was.

"I hed orter like him best of all," she thought reproachfully.

Two or three days later Pete Noyes came to the house.

"Hello, Amarilly! I ain't seen yer in so long I'd fergit how you looked. Say, why didn't you ever fix yer hair that way afore? It looks swell, even if it is red!"

"I am older now," she explained in superior, lofty tones, "and of course

I hev to think more about my looks than I used ter."

He gazed at her with such ardent admiration that she was seized with an impulse to don her white dress and impress his young fancy still further.

"He ain't wuth it, though," her sober second thought decided.

"What does yer think I come fer, Amarilly?"

"I dunno, 'less Mr. Vedder sent you."

"He did, sorter. You see, I'm invited to one of them kind of parties whar you dress up ter be the name of a book. One of the stock company is givin' it fer her kids. I don't know the name of any book except Diamond Dick and The Curse of Gold, and I didn't know how to rig up fer them. I went to Vedder, and he sez thar's a book what's called The Little Minister, and I could rent yer surplus and tog out in it. He said you would take tucks in it fer me."

"Sure I will. I'll fix it now while you wait, Pete."

"Say, Amarilly, I thought as how, seein' we are both in the perfesshun, sorter, you'd come down on your price."

"Sure thing, Pete. I won't charge you nothin' fer it."

"Yes; I wanter pay. I'll tell you what, Amarilly, couldn't you take it out in gum? I hed a hull lot left over when the theayter shut down. It'll git stale ef I keep it much longer, and I'd like to git some of it offen my hands."

"Sure, I will, Pete. We all like gum, and we can't afford to buy it very often. That'll be dandy."

Thus it was that for the next fortnight the Jenkins family revelled in the indulgence of a hitherto denied but dearly prized luxury. Their jaws worked constantly and joyously, although differently. Mrs. Jenkins, by reason of depending upon her third set of teeth, chewed cautiously and with camel-like precision. The Boarder, having had long practice in the art, craunched at railway speed. The older boys munched steadily and easily, while Bud and Bobby pecked intermittently in short nibbles. Amarilly had the "star method," which they all vainly tried to emulate. At short and regular intervals a torpedo-like report issued from the gum as she snapped her teeth down upon it. Cory kept hers strung out elastically from her mouth, occasionally rolling it back.

The liberal supply of the luxury rapidly diminished, owing to the fact that Iry swallowed his allowance after ineffectual efforts to retain it in his mouth, and then like Oliver Twist pleaded for more.

"I declare fer it!" remarked Mrs. Hudgers to Amarilly. "That child's insides will all be stuck together. I should think yer ma would be afeard to let him chaw so much."

"He's ateethin', and it sorter soothes his gums," explained Amarilly.

During the summer season, Pete had pursued his profession at a vaudeville theatre, and one day, not long after his literary representation, he came to Amarilly with some good tidings.

"I hev another job fer yer surplus. Down to the vawdyville they're goin' to put on a piece what has a preacher in it, and I tole them about yer surplus, and the leadin' man, who is to be the preacher, says 'twould lend to the settin's to wear it. I told him mebby you'd let him hev the use on it fer a week fer five dollars. He said he could buy the stuff and make a dozen fer

72

that price, but they gotter start the piece to-night so that'd be no time to make one. I'll take it down to them to-night."

This was the longest and most remunerative act of the surplice, and served to pay for a very long accruing milk bill. When the engagement at the vaudeville ended, the Boarder came to the rescue.

"Thar's a friend of mine what brakes, and he wants the surplus to wear to a maskyrade. I told him he could go as a preacher. He's asavin' to git married, so he don't want to give much."

"He shell hev it fer a quarter," said Amarilly, friend to all lovers, "and I'll lend him a mask. I hev one the property man at the theayter give me."

CHAPTER XII

"I wonder," meditated Gus, "where the surplus will land next?"

"It has been most everywhere except to the police court," said Bobby.

"'Spect 'twill land there next!"

His prophecy was fulfilled. Mrs. Jenkins washed the lucrative garment late one afternoon and left it on the line all night. The next morning, to the great consternation of the family and the wild distress of Amarilly, the beloved surplice, that friend of friends in time of need, had vanished. Other clotheslines in the vicinity had also been deprived of their burdens, and a concerted complaint was made to the police, who promptly located the offender and brought him summarily to trial. Mrs. Jenkins was subpoenaed as a witness, which caused quite a ripple of excitement in the family. Divided between dread of appearing in public and pride at the importance with which she was regarded by her little flock, Mrs. Jenkins was quite upset by the occasion. She hadn't attended a function for so long that her costuming therefor was of more concern than had been Amarilly's church raiment.

Mrs. Hudgers loaned her mourning bonnet and veil, which was adjusted at half mast. They appeared in direct contradiction to the skirt of bilious green she wore, but the Jenkinses were as unconventional in attire as they were in other things.

The family attended the trial en masse, and were greatly elated at the prominence their mother had attained. The culprit was convicted and the surplice duly restored. The misfortune was not without profit. Mrs. Jenkins received thirty-five cents as a witness fee.

They had managed to pay their household expenses through the summer, but when the rent for August was due there was not quite enough cash on hand to meet this important item of expenditure. Noting the troubled brows of Mrs. Jenkins and Amarilly at breakfast time, the Boarder insisted on knowing the cause.

"We're broke, and the rent's overdue," tersely explained Amarilly.

"I'm broke, too," sighed the Boarder, "except what I've got in the savin's bank towards—"

"Lily Rose," suggested Amarilly softly.

"Yes," he admitted, with a beaming look. "But when I go broke, all other things failin', I allers tackle a pawnbroker."

"We ain't got nothin' to pawn," sighed Amarilly.

She recalled the lace waist, but that, like the Lily Rose fund, was sacred. There was always, to-day, yesterday, and forever, the surplice, and her scruples regarding that article had of necessity become case- hardened; still, Amarilly hesitated. A pawnshop seemed lower than a police court.

"It's been everywhere else," she said loudly to the accusing, still, small voice, "and it might jest as well go the limit. 'T won't bring much, but 'twill help."

Through byways and highways Amarilly sought the region of the three-balled porticoes. The shop of one Max Solstein attracted her, and she entered his open door. Max, rat-eyed and frog-mouthed, came forward propitiatingly.

"What'll you gimme on this?" came with directness from the small importuner.

He took the garment, shook it, and held it up for falcon-gaze inspection.

"Not worth much. A quarter of a dollar."

Amarilly snatched it from his grasp and fled. Not because of his low-figured offer; she had fully expected to have to "beat him up." But when she had entered, a youth who had all the recognized earmarks of a reporter was lounging in the doorway. At sight of the uplifted garment he had come eagerly forward, scenting a story. She knew his kind from snatches of conversation she had heard between the leading lady and Lord Algernon. In the lore of the stage at Barlow's, reporters were "hovering vultures" who always dropped down when least wanted, and they had a way of dragging to light the innermost thoughts of their victims.

"You read your secrets," Lord Algernon had dramatically declared, "in blazoned headlines."

Hitherto Amarilly had effectually silenced her instinctive rebellion against the profaning of St. John's surplice, but she had reached the limit. No Max Solstein, no threatening landlord, no ruthless reporter should thrust the sacred surplice into the publicity of print.

She darted from the shop, the reporter right at her heels, but the chasing of his covey to corner was not easily accomplished. He was a newly fledged reporter, and Amarilly had all the instinct of the lowly for localities. She turned and doubled and dodged successfully. By a course circuitous she returned to Hebrew haunts, this time to seek, one Abram Canter, a little wizened, gnome-like Jew. Assuring herself that there was no other than the proprietor within, Amarilly entered and handed over the surplice for appraisal.

Once more the garment was held aloft. At that psychological moment an elderly man of buxom build, benevolent in mien, and with smooth, long hair that had an upward rolling tendency at the ends, looked in the shop as he was passing. He halted, hesitated, and then entered. Of him, however, Amarilly felt no apprehension.

"Looks like Quaker Oats, or mebby it's the Jack of Spades," she thought after a searching survey.

"My child, is that yours?" he asked of Amarilly, indicating the garment by a protesting forefinger.

"Sure thing!" she acknowledged frankly.

"Where did you get it?"

If he had been a young man, Amarilly would have cheerfully reminded him that it was none of his business, but, a respecter of age, she loftily informed him that it had been "give to her."

"By whom?" he persisted.

Perceiving her reluctance to answer, he added gently:

"I am a bishop of the Episcopal Church, and I cannot endure to see a surplice in such a place as this."

A bishop! This was worse than a reporter even. St. John would surely hear of it! But she felt that an explanation was due the calling of her interlocutor.

She lifted righteous eyes to his.

"My mother works for one of the churches, and the minister, he give us this to cut up into clo'es fer the chillern, but we didn't cut it up. I'm agoin' to leave it here till the rent's paid, and we git the money to take it outen hock."

The bishop's eyes softened, and lost their look of shocked dignity.

"I will advance you the money," he offered. "I would much prefer to do so than to have it left here. How much money do you need to pay your rent?"

"We need five dollars," said Amarilly, "to pay the balance of it. But I wouldn't take it from you. I ain't no beggar. I don't believe, nuther," she continued, half to herself, "that Mr. St. John would like it."

"Who is Mr. St. John?" he asked curiously. "I know of no such rector in this diocese. My child, you have an honest face. Since you won't accept a gift of money, I will lend, you the amount. I want you to tell me all about yourself and this surplice."

"Well, mebby he'd want me to," reflected Amarilly.

"Gimme back that surplus," she said to the Jew, who seemed loath to relinquish his booty.

As she walked up the street with the bishop, she frankly related the family history and the part Mr. Meredith and the surplice had played therein.

The bishop had generous instincts, and a desire to reach the needy directly instead of through the medium of institutions, but he had never known just how to approach them. His presence in this unknown part of the city had been unpremeditated, but he welcomed the chance that had led his steps hither to perform an errand of mercy. He handed Amarilly five dollars, and wrote down her address. He was most reluctant to receive the surplice as security, but Amarilly's firm insistence was not to be overcome. She returned home, rejoicing in the knowledge that she had the price of their happy home in her pocket. The bishop had given her his card, which she laid in a china saucer with other bits of pasteboard she had collected from Derry Phillips, Mr. Vedder, and Pete Noyes. The saucer adorned a small stand in the dining-room part of the house.

"It's the way Mrs. Hubbleston kep' her keerds," Amarilly explained to the family.

Meantime the bishop was walking in an opposite direction toward his home, wondering if he should find he was mistaken in his estimate of human nature; and a query arose in his mind as to what he should do with the surplice if it were left on his hands.

CHAPTER XIII

Bud sat in the park,—Clothes-line Park, Amarilly had dubbed it—one Monday afternoon, singing a song of gladness. The park was confined by a clothes-line stretched between three tottering poles and the one solitary poplar tree of the Jenkins estate. The line was hung with white linen garments, and smaller articles adorned the grass plot within the park.

This to Bud was the most beautiful spot in the world. He looked up into the sapphire blue of the sky flecked with soft patches of white, then down upon the waving grass latticed by sun and shade; he listened to the soothing rustle of the poplar leaves, the soft flapping of linen in the breeze, the birds in the tree tops, and felt his heart and throat bursting with all the harmony and melody about him. Not always was Bud's refrain one of joy. There were songs of sorrow on the damp days when the washings must be dried within the house, and he could not venture forth because he still was regarded as the delicate one of the family. There were days, too, when the number of garments was not adequate to complete the boundary to the park, and that meant less to eat and worry about the rent and a harassed look in his mother's anxious eyes.

But there was no sob in Bud's song this afternoon. The clothes had been hung out unusually early, and were nearly dry, so his mother had brought out her little lean-back rocker and sat beside him for a few moments to listen to his carol and to hark back to the days when his lusty-voiced father had sung to her in the shadows of a vine clad porch.

It was not upon Amarilly, the sharer of her burdens, nor upon the baby that Mrs. Jenkins lavished her tenderness. Bud crept closest because he had been the one most dependent upon her care.

When the little singer ceased, the mother arose and unpinned the garments, carrying them in armfuls to the huge basket in the middle of the park. Bud watched her thin, fatigued hands as they performed their accustomed task, and a sudden inspiration came to him. His future field of labor had troubled him. Now his way seemed clear. He stepped nimbly to the grass plot and gathered up the pieces spread thereon.

"Ma," he said, as they met at the basket, "I've jest thought what I kin do, when I grow up, to support you."

"What is it, Bud?" she asked interestedly.

"The teacher said we must plan to do what we knew the most about. I know more about washin' than anything else."

"You'd orter," she replied with a sigh.

"I kin run a laundry," he declared.

"That would be a fine business."

Happy in the hope of this new horoscope, Bud resumed his seat in the amphitheatre, and in a voice of clarion clearness ecstatically rendered one of the hymns he had learned at St. Mark's. Ever since he had become a member of the choir, Clothes-line Park had rung with echoes of the Jubilate and Venite instead of the popular old-time school airs. The wringer was turned to the tune of a Te Deum, the clothes were rubbed to the rhythm of a Benedictus, and the floor mopped to the melody of a Magnificat.

On the happy, by-gone Thursdays, cloistered by snow-white surplices, with the little chorister enthroned in the midst, Clothes-line Park had seemed a veritable White Chapel.

Bud was snatched from his carols by the arrival of Amarilly, who was far too practical to hearken to hymns when there was work to be performed.

"I got the money Miss Ormsby's owed us so long," she announced in a tone of satisfaction, "and that jest makes up the money to git back the surplus. I'll give you carfare one way, Bud, and you must go to the bishop's and git it. I'm too beat to go. I've walked most five miles sence dinner."

Bud was scoured and brushed, the pocket of his blouse tagged with a five-dollar bill carefully secured by a safety pin, and he started on his way for the address Amarilly had given him. He stopped at the corner drug store to spend his car-fare for an ice-cream soda.

When the lad's quest was repeated to the bishop by his housekeeper, he instructed her to send Bud up to the library, being kindly-disposed towards all boy-kind. While he was questioning his young visitor, the organ of Grace Church, which was next to the bishop's house, pealed forth, and a man's voice began to chant a selection from an oratorio Bud had learned at St. Mark's. A high, childish soprano voice was essaying to carry the sustained note an octave above the man's voice; once it sharped.

"Oh!" shuddered Bud in dismay. "He can't keep the tune."

"He isn't our regular soloist," explained the bishop apologetically. "He is ill, and this boy is trying to learn the part for an organ recital to be given next week."

Again the choirmaster's voice, patient and wearied, began the refrain. Instinctively Bud's little chest swelled, and involuntarily his clear, high treble took the note and sustained it without break through the measures, and then triumphantly broke into the solo. The bishop's eyes shone.

"Come," he said, rising and going towards the door, "come with me."

Wonderingly and obediently, Bud followed him into the church and up to the organ where the choirmaster sat.

"This is one of the boys from St. Mark's. Try him on the solo. He just sang it for me."

"I thought I heard it sung just now, but I feared it was only an echo of my dreams. Let me hear you again, my lad."

Easily and confidently Bud attacked the high C in alt. At the end of the solo, the long-suffering choirmaster looked as if he were an Orpheus, who had found his Eurydice.

"Who taught you to sing that solo?" he demanded.

"My school teacher. She is studying fer an opery singer, and she helps me with my Sunday singing."

"I thought the style was a little florid for the organist of St. Mark's," said the choirmaster whimsically. "My boy, if you will sing it for us at the recital as well as you did just now, you shall have ten dollars."

The laundry now loomed as a fixed star in Bud's firmament. When he went home and told his mother the good news she moved joyfully among her mops and tubs. The turn of the wringer never seemed so easy, and she frequently paused in the rubbing of a soaped garment to wring the suds from her swollen hands and listen anew to the recital of Bud's call upon the bishop and the choirmaster of Grace Church.

CHAPTER XIV

The next day the flood-tide of the Jenkins's fortunes bid fair to flow to fullness. Word came to the little home that Mr. Meredith had returned to the city and desired the laundry work to be resumed. Bud was summoned to choir practice the following Friday, and Miss King sent her chauffeur with a fair-sized washing.

"Everything comes so to onct, it takes your breath away," said Amarilly, quite overcome by this renewal of commercial activity, "and next thing I know,"—there her heart gave a deer-like leap—"Mr. Derry'll be hum, and sendin' fer me. Then we'll all be earnin' excep' Gus."

At the end of the week Amarilly eagerly went to deliver the washings at the rectory and Miss King's, but in both instances she was doomed to disappointment, as her friends were not in.

"I'll go to church and see 'em," she resolved.

This time her raiment was very simple, but more effective than upon the occasion of her previous attendance.

Before Amarilly's artistic temperament was awakened by the atmosphere of the studio, she had been wont to array herself in things convenient without regard to color or style, believing herself to be hopelessly homely and beyond the aid of personal adornment; but since Derry had praised her hair, she had scrupulously cared for it and allowed no conflicting color in proximity thereto. On this occasion she fastened it with the black velvet bows, and arrayed herself in the white dress Mrs. Jimmels had given her.

"I declar, Amarilly," exclaimed her mother, "I believe you're agrowin' purty!"

Amarilly's eyes danced, and she gave her mother a spontaneous and rewarding hug.

She didn't do her own ushering this time, and was consequently seated most inconspicuously near the entrance. Her heart beat rapturously at the sight of John Meredith in the pulpit.

"His vacation didn't freshen him up much," she thought, after a shrewd glance. "He's paler and don't look real peart. Sorter like Bud arter he got up from the fever."

Her attention was diverted from the rector by the vision of Colette coming down the aisle. The change in her appearance was even more startling to the little anxious-eyed girl than in John's case. There were violet shadows under the bright eyes, a subtle, subdued air about her fresh young beauty that had banished the little touch of wilfulness. As soon as she was seated, which was after the service had begun, she became entirely absorbed in her prayer-book.

"Vacation ain't agreed with her, nuther," pondered Amarilly perplexedly.

She turned her gaze again to John, who was sitting back of the choir, while his "understudy" conducted the service. His face was shaded by his hand, but Amarilly's gimlet glance noted that he frequently sent a fleeting, troubled look toward the King pew.

"Thar's something up atwixt 'em," deduced Amarilly, "and they air both too proud to say nuthin' about it to the other."

John's sermon was on the strength that renunciation brings, and the duty of learning resignation. There was a pervasive note of sadness in his deliverance of the theme, and Amarilly felt her joyousness in the return of her friends slipping from her.

She went out of church somewhat depressed, but was cheered by the handclasp of the rector and his earnest assurance that he would see her very soon. While he was saying this, Colette slipped past without vouchsafing so much as a glance in their direction. Hurt through and through, the little girl walked sadly to the pavement with head and eyes downcast.

"Amarilly," dulcetly spoke a well-loved voice.

Her eyes turned quickly. Colette stood at the curb, her hand on the door of the electric.

"I waited to take you home, dear. Why, what's the matter, Amarilly?

Tears?"

"I thought you wan't goin' to speak to me," said Amarilly, as she stepped into the brougham and took the seat beside Colette.

"I didn't want to interrupt you and Mr. Meredith, but it's a wonder I knew you. You look so different. You have grown so tall, and what a beautiful dress! Who showed you how to fix your hair so artistically? I never realized you had such beautiful hair, child!"

"I didn't nuther, till he told me."

"Who, Amarilly? Lord Algernon?"

"No!" scoffed Amarilly, suddenly realizing that her former hero had toppled from his pedestal in her thoughts. "'Tain't him. It's a new friend I have made. An artist."

"Oh, Amarilly, you have such distinguished acquaintances! All in the profession, too. Tell me who the artist is."

"Mr. Derry Phillips. I cleaned his rooms, and he took me to lunch. We ate things like we had to your house."

"Derry Phillips, the talented young artist! Why, Amarilly, girls are tumbling over each other trying to get attention from him, and he took you to luncheon! Where?"

"To Carter's, and I'm to serve his breakfast and take care of his rooms, and he showed me how to fix my hair and to say 'can' and 'ate.' He's fired the woman what red his rooms."

"'Merely Mary Ann,'" murmured Colette.

"No," said Amarilly positively. "Her name is Miss O'Leary, and she didn't clean the mopboards."

Colette's gay laughter pealed forth.

"Amarilly, this is the first time, I've laughed this summer, but I must explain something to you. The housekeeper told me that all the children had scarlet fever and were quarantined a long time after we left. I wish I

85

had known it and thought more about you, but—I've had troubles of my own. How did you manage so long with nothing coming in?"

"It was purty hard, but we fetched it," sighed Amarilly, thinking of the struggles, "We're doin' fine now again."

"But, tell me; how did you buy food and things when none of you were working?"

"When your ten dollars was gone, we spent his'n."

"Whose?"

"Mr. Meredith's. He sent us a ten, too."

"Oh!" replied Colette frigidly.

"Then the Boarder give us all he hed. Arterwards come dark days until Mr. Vedder sent us a fiver.—Then thar was an orful day when thar wa'n't a cent and we didn't know whar to turn, and then—It saved us."

"It? What?"

"The surplus. Mr. St. John's surplus. It brung in lots."

"Why, what do you mean, Amarilly?"

"You see 'twas at our house when Iry was fust took sick—same as the waist you gimme was. They couldn't nuther on 'em be sent hum till they was fumygated. Then Mrs. Winders said as how he, Mr. St. John, said as how we was to keep it and cut it up fer the chillern, but we didn't."

"Oh, Amarilly," asked Colette faintly, "do you mean to tell me that the surplice was never delivered to Mr. Meredith?"

"No. Gus didn't take it that night, and in the mornin' when Iry was took it was too late. And then when it got fumygated, Mr. St. John had gone away and he left word we was to keep it."

The transformation in Colette's mobile face during this explanation was rapid and wonderful. With a radiant smile she stopped the brougham and put her arms impulsively about Amarilly.

"Oh, Amarilly, I'm so happy, and I've had such a wretched summer! Now, we will go right to your house and you'll let me see the surplice." Amarilly looked surprised.

"Why, yes, you can see it, of course, though it ain't no diffrent from his other ones."

"Oh yes it is! Far, far different, Amarilly. It has a history."

"Yes, I guess it has," laughed Amarilly, "It's been goin' some these last two months!"

"Why, what do you mean, Amarilly? and I forgot in my excitement to ask how it helped you. But first tell me. You know there is a pocket in it?"

"Yes, Miss King."

"Have you noticed anything in the pocket?"

"Never looked onct. But then if thar was 'twould hev come out in the wash. It's been did up heaps of times. You see, rentin' it out so much—"

"Renting it out!"

Amarilly gave a graphic account of the adventures of the errant garment to date. Meanwhile Colette's countenance underwent kaleidoscopic changes.

"Amarilly," she asked faintly, "have you the addresses of all those people to whom you rented it?"

"Yes; I keep books now, and I put it down in my day ledger the way the

Boarder showed me."

"There was something—of mine—in—that pocket. Will you ask your mother to look for it, and hunt the house over for it?"

Amarilly, greatly distressed at the loss, promised faithfully to do so.

CHAPTER XV

As soon as Amarilly had been deposited at her door, Colette tore a leaf from the tablet reposing in its silver case, hastily wrote a few lines, and then ran her brougham at full speed back to St. Mark's. A chorister was just coming out.

"Walter!" she called.

The lad came down to the curb.

"Will you please take this to Mr. Meredith? He is probably in the

Sunday-school now."

"Sure. Will you wait for an answer, Miss King?".

"No, thank you, Walter."

She rode home and waited anxiously for the personal answer to her note, which came with most unclerical alacrity.

"Colette," he said, his voice tense, "if you knew what your little note meant! Did—"

"Wait until I explain, John. I must tell you about the surplice."

She repeated Amarilly's account of the peregrinations of the robe.

"Well?" he asked bewildered, "I don't see what that has to do with—"

"Everything. There was something of mine—" she turned a deep crimson— "in the pocket of that surplice."

"Yours! Why, how did it get there, Colette? Was it—"

"I am not going to tell you—not until I have it back. Oh, I could die of shame when I think who may have found it. You must get it."

"Colette," he answered gravely, "the surplice must have passed through many hands, but if it is possible to trace this—article, I will do so. Still, how can I make inquiries unless I know what it is?"

"You can ask them, each and all, if they found anything in the pocket," she replied. "And you must tell them you left it there."

"And you won't trust me, Colette? Not after my long unhappy summer. And won't you give me an answer now to the note I wrote you last spring?"

"No; I won't tell you anything! Not until you find that."

"Be reasonable, Colette."

His choice of an adjective was most unfortunate for his cause. It was the word of words that Colette detested; doubtless because she had been so often entreated to cultivate that quality.

"I will not," she answered, "if to tell you is being reasonable. I must have it back. I think no one will really know to whom it belongs, though they may guess. You must, assume the ownership."

"I certainly shall, if it can be found," he assured her.

Seeing the utter futility of changing her mood, he took his departure; perhaps a little wiser if not quite so sad as he had been before he saw her. The next morning he called upon Amarilly, whom he found alone with Iry.

"I am very sorry to learn that you had such a hard summer," he said kindly, "and I regret that I didn't know more about your affairs before I left the city, but I was too absorbed, I fear, in my own troubles."

"How did you hear about us?" she asked curiously.

"From Miss King."

"Oh," said Amarilly happily, imagining that their trouble must have been patched up. Then another thought occurred to her which gave her a little heart palpitation. With intense anxiety depicted on her lineaments she asked tremulously: "Did she tell you about the surplus?"

"Amarilly," and the tone was so reassuring that the little wrinkles of anxiety vanished, "when I gave you the surplice, I gave it to you unconditionally, and I am very glad that you put it to profit. But, you know, as Miss King told you, that there was something of value—of importance—in that pocket; something that must be found. My happiness depends entirely upon its recovery. Now, she tells me that you can give me the names and addresses of all the people through whose hands it passed."

"Sure thing!" she replied with business-like alacrity. "You see the Boarder has been larnin' me bookkeepin', and so I keep all our accounts now in a big book the grocer give me."

She produced a large, ledger-like book and laid it on the table for his inspection. He examined her system of bookkeeping with interest. Under the head of "Cr.," which she explained to him meant "brung in," was "Washins," "Boarder," "Flamingus," "Milt," "Bobby," "Bud." Below each of these subheads were dates and accounts. The page opposite, headed "Dr.," she translated, "means paid out."

She turned a few leaves, and in big letters he read the word "Surplus."

"This bein' a sort of extry account, the Boarder said to run it as a special and keep it seprut. If you'll set down, I'll read offer to you whar it has went."

She began to read laboriously and slowly from the book, adding explanatory notes in glib tones.

"'July 8. Mister Carrul, tenner, 1 doller. Pade.' He's the tenor, you know, to Grace Church. He wanted it to sing in at a sacred concert. His was too short or too long.

"'July 11. Miss Lyte and Miss Bobson. 'Tablos. 1 doller. Pade.' Mr.

Carul knows where they live. 'Twaz him as got the job fer me.

"'July 15 to July 19. The Beehive. 3 dollers and 1/2 Pade.' That's a bargain store down in our parts. I went in fer to git Bud a cap and I hearn the clerk askin' the boss about fixin' up a winder show with wax figgers fer a weddin'. I step up to him and ask him if he kep surpluses, and he sez as he didn't. I told him I could rent him one to put on the minister, and he hedn't thought fer to hev it an Episcopal show, but he sed he'd do it fer an ad fer his white goods. He wouldn't stand fer no dollar a day. He beat me down to three-fifty, but he throwed in a cap fer Bud.

"Next come Mrs. Hudgers. I didn't put it down in the ledger, though, cause it didn't bring nuthin' but a pan of doughnuts. Her son Hallie died, and he didn't hev no nice clo'es ter be laid out in, and she was agoin' to hev quite a funyral, so jest afore folks come, she slipped the surplus on ter him over his old clo'es, and then when 'twas over, she took it offen him again. He made a swell lookin' corpse. Bein' a neighbor we didn't go fer to ask her nuthin', but she give us the nut cakes. They give her dyspepsy, anyhow."

The muscles of John Meredith's face grew rigid in his endeavor to maintain a serious expression. He had taken out a notebook at the beginning of the interview to jot down the addresses, but he copied Amarilly's comments as well, for the future entertainment of Colette.

"'July 25 and 26. Mr. Derry Phillips, The Navarre. 2 dollers. Pade.' He paints picters. He painted the surplus onto a man playin' on a orgin."

She hesitated a moment, and then continued: "I'm agoin' to work reg'lur fer him instead of to the theayter. I'm agoin' to git his breakfast and clean his rooms. He'll pay me the same as I got. He's a sort of eddicatin' me too."

"Why, how is that, Amarilly?" asked John in perplexity.

"He larnt me not to say 'et' and 'kin.'"

The rector's eyes twinkled.

"And," pursued Amarilly, after another moment of hesitancy, "he's larnt me how to fix my hair. He says red hair is beautiful! He took me to a restyrant."

John looked troubled at this statement, and felt that his call at the studio would now be for a double purpose.

"'July 27,'" resumed Amarilly. "'The Boarder. 25 cents. Pade.'"

"Why, what possible use could he have for a surplice?"

"He's akeepin' company with a young gal—Lily Rose—and she wanted his likeness tooken sorter fancy-like, so he wuz took in the surplus, and he got himself framed in a gilt and shell frame, and she hez it ahangin' over her bed. I didn't want no pay from him, cause he give us his money when yours and Miss King's was gone, but he says as how it might bring him luck in gittin' her, so I took a quarter of a dollar."

"'July 29. Mister Vergil Washington. Reckter Colered Church. 1 doller. Pade.' Some one stole his'n off en the clo'es-line, and he only hed one.

"'July 31. Widder Hubbleston, 56 Wilkins St. 1 Doller. Pade.' She got married by an Episcopal minister, and he furgot his surplus, and that was all she hed hired him fer, so she rented our'n fer him, and Mr. Jimmels, her new husband, took it outen the minister's pay. Somethin' allers goes wrong to her weddin's."

"Does she have them often?" interrupted John gravely.

"Quite frequent." "'Aug. 3, Mister Vedder, Ticket Seller to the

Theayter. 1 doller. Pade.' He wore it to a sheet and piller case party.

I didn't want fer to take nuthin' from him, cause he give us money when

we hed the fever, but he wouldn't hev it that way.

"'Aug. 5. Pete Noyes. Gum.' He's the boy what sells gum to the theayter. He was agoin' to a party whar you hev to be the name of a book. He wore the surplus so his name was the Little Minister. We took it out in gum — spruce and pepsin. Iry swallered his'n every time, and Miss Hudgers was afeard he'd be stuck together inside.

"'Aug. 9-23. Vawdevil Theayter. 5 dollers. Pade.' They put it on fer a sketch.

"'Aug. 25. Mister Cotter. 25 cents. Pade.' He's a brakeman friend of the

Boarder. He wore it to a maskyrade.

"'Aug. 27. Poleece. 35 cents. Pade.'"

"Police!" ejaculated John faintly.

"Some one swiped it offen our clo'es-line, and when the police ketched the thief, we was subpenyed, or ma was. She got thirty-five cents, and all on us 'cept Iry went to hear her."

"'Aug, 29. Bishop Thurber. 5 dollers. Pade.'"

"Bishop Thurber!" the name was repeated with the force of an expletive.

"Seems to mind that more'n he did the police," thought Amarilly.

"It's quite a story," she explained, "and though it was orful at the beginnin' it come out all right, jest as the plays all do. I jest thought, I shouldn't hev put that down in the account, cause we give back the five, so we didn't make nuthin' in a way. We wuz dead broke. I suppose," she ruminated, "you don't know jest how orful it is to be that."

"I don't, Amarilly, from my own experience," replied John sympathetically, "but I can imagine how terrible it must be, and I am very sorry — "

"Well, as long as it come out all right, it don't make no difference. We'd got to pay our rent or else git put out, and I was up a stump till the Boarder said to tackle a pawnshop. I didn't hev nuthin' but the surplus to pawn, and I hated to pawn it on your account."

"I don't care, my child," was the fervent assurance, "where you took it as long as it helped you in your troubles."

"Well, I was in a pawnshop, and the man was holdin' it up, and the bishop went by, and when he seen what it was he come in, and asked me all about it, and I told him. He took it worse than you do that I would pawn it, and to save it he lent me five dollers. Course I made him take the surplus till I hed the money to git it outen hock, and when we was able to pay fer it, Bud went arter it. Thar was a boy practicin' at the church next door, and he warn't singin' it right, and Bud he couldn't keep still noway, so he up and sings the soler, and when the man at the orgin hearn him, he fired the boy what was tryin' to sing, and hired Bud in his place. He's agoin' to sing to a recital at Grace Church day arter to-morrer, and git ten dollers. And we air goin' to make Bud bank all he gits cause he ain't so strong as the rest of us. He may need it some time. That's all the places the surplus went to. I guess I'll go outen the costumin' business now, 'cause I'll be startin' in with Mr. Derry soon."

CHAPTER XVI

There was one little ominous cloud in the serene sky of Mrs. Jenkins's happiness. She had nothing suitable for the occasion of the organ recital in the way of wearing apparel.

"I feel as if gloves was due you, Bud," she lamented, "but I kin't afford 'em. I guess I kin put my hands under my mantilly, though, and folks won't know."

"She'd orter hev 'em, and she'd orter hev a new hat, too," reflected Bud, and his song became a requiem. He manfully resolved to sacrifice his future to present needs and curtail the laundry fund. After some meditation he called upon the bishop, and asked if he might have an advance of half the amount he would receive for his solo.

The bishop readily assented, but sought the reason for the request.

"My mother is comin' to the recital, but she ain't got no fixin's. I'm goin' to buy her a hat."

"I am glad you think of your mother, my lad, but it would be well to let some older person select it for you. My housekeeper—"

Bud's refusal was emphatic. He knew the kind of hat his mother wanted, and he had noted her quickly suppressed look of disappointment at the sombre hat donated by Mrs. Hudgers on the day of the police-court attendance.

Upon receiving the five dollars he went directly to the Fashion Emporium, where the windows were filled with a heterogeneous assortment of gayly trimmed hats, marked enticingly with former and present prices.

"I want a hat kivered with flowers," he announced.

"Who for?" asked the young saleswoman.

"For my mother."

"How would you like a nice flower toque like this?" displaying a headgear of modest forget-me-nots.

"That's all faded. Ain't you got any red flowers? If you haven't, I know a store where they keep 'em."

The girl instantly sacrificed her ideas of what was fitting to the certainty of a sale, and quickly produced a hat of green foliage from which rose long-stemmed, nodding red poppies, "a creation marked down to three-ninety-eight," she informed him.

"That's the kind! I'll take it and a pair of white gloves, too, if you've got some big ones fer a dollar."

Bud hastened home with his purchases. His mother was quite overcome by the sight of such finery.

"I never thought to be dressed up again," she exclaimed on the eventful night, "No one has bought me nuthin' to wear sence your pa died. I feel like I was some one outen a book."

The entire family, save Iry, who was put to bed at a neighbor's, went to the recital. The Boarder took Lily Rose, who was quite flustered at her first appearance with the family.

John and Colette occupied a pew directly opposite the family. Mr. Vedder and Pete were also in attendance.

When the bishop came from the vestry and walked down the aisle to his pew, his eyes fell upon the worn, seamed face of Bud's mother, the weary patient eyes in such odd contrast to the youthful turban with its smartly dancing flowers. Something stirred in his well-regulated heart, and he carefully wiped his glasses.

At the signal from the choirmaster for the solo of the oratorio, Bud arose. An atom of a boy he looked in the vast, vaulted chancel, and for the first time he knew fear at the thought of singing. It was a terrible thing, after all, to face this sea of staring, dancing people. As lightning reaches to steel, the gay poppies nodding so nervously above his mother's white, anxious face sought the courage place within, and urged him on. He felt himself back in Clothes-line Park, alone with his mother and the blue sky.

The little figure filled itself with a long, deep breath. The high, clear note merged into one with the notes of the chorus. It touched the tones of the accompaniment in harmony true, and swelled into grand, triumphant music.

"He looks like he did arter the fever," thought Amarilly anxiously.

When he came down the aisle with the choir, the ethereal look had left his face, and he was again a happy little boy. He gave his mother a gay nod, and bestowed a wink upon the Boarder. He waited outside and the family wended their way homeward.

There had not been time to bring in the clothes before leaving, but a willing neighborhood had guarded the premises for them, so Clothes-line Park was shrouded in a whiteness that looked ghostly in the moonlight.

They made quite an affair of the evening in honor of Bud's song, and their introduction to Lily Rose. There were fried sausages, coffee, sandwiches, and pork cake.

"The organist told me," announced Bud at supper, "that he was agoin' to train my voice, and I could be soloist at Grace Church and git five dollars a Sunday, and after a while I could git ten."

"You'll be a millynaire," prophesied Bobby in awed tones.

"Guess we'll be on Easy Street now," shouted Cory.

"We won't be nuthin' of the kind," snapped Amarilly. "It's agoin' to all be banked fer Bud."

"I guess," said Bud, in his quiet, little old-man way, "I'm the one to hev the say. I'm agoin' to give ma two dollars a week and bank the rest."

Meanwhile John was having an uncomfortable time as he walked home with Colette. He had started on the trail of the surplice the day before. The "tenner" and the young ladies who had given the tableaux had been interviewed, but in neither case had the mysterious pocket been discovered. To-day he had visited the Beehive, but no one in the store had paid any attention to the pocket, or knew of its existence. Colette remained obdurate to his pleadings. She assumed that he was entirely to blame for the loss, and seemed to take a gleeful delight in showing him how perverse and wilful she could be. To-night he found himself less able than usual to cope with her caprices, so he began to talk of impersonal matters and dwelt upon the beauties of Bud's voice, and the astonishing way in which it had developed.

She admitted that Bud's voice was indeed wonderful, but maintained that Mrs. Jenkins's poppy hat and white gloves had been far surpassing in the way of surprises.

"Did you ever, John, see anything more shoutingly funny?"

"It wasn't funny, Colette," he said wistfully, and he proceeded to relate the history of the hat as he had heard it from the bishop that day.

And though in the depths of her heart Colette was touched by the pathos of the purchase, she must needs tread again the feminine labyrinth instead of following the more natural and open path.

"Who was the young girl with the Boarder?" John next vouchsafed.

"Why, Lily Rose, of course. The Lily for whom he 'sot for his likeness in the surplus.' That awful surplice," she burst forth in irritation at the mere mention of the unfortunate word. "Some of these people must have it. John, you don't half try to find it."

"I am following out the list in order," he assured her. "I shall go to see Mrs. Hudgers to-morrow."

"And the next one to her," reminded Colette, "is Derry Phillips, Amarilly's new benefactor. She told me to-day that she had a note from him, asking her to begin work at the studio in a few days."

"I have a double duty in my call there," said John didactically. "If he is like some of the young artists I know, his studio will hardly be a proper place for Amarilly."

"As it happens," returned Colette coldly, "Derry Phillips, for all his nonsense, is reported to be a true gentleman; but it would make no difference with Amarilly if he were not. Her inherent goodness would counteract the evil of any atmosphere. She can take care of his rooms until she is a little older. Then she can become a model."

"Colette!" he exclaimed protestingly.

"Why not?" she returned. "Why shouldn't Amarilly be a model, or go on the stage? Neither place would be below her station in life."

John sought refuge in utter silence which admonished and exasperated

Colette far more than any reproof would have done.

"You might as well go, if you have nothing to say," she remarked stiffly, as he lingered in the portico, evidently expecting an invitation to enter.

"I have too much to say, Colette."

Her sidelong glance noted his dejection, and her flagging spirits rose again.

"Too much, indeed, when you are so critical of what I say!"

"Colette, hear me!"

"No, I won't listen—never when you preach!"

"I don't mean to preach, Colette, but don't you think—"

"Good night, John," she said, smiling.

"Good night!" he echoed dolefully, but making no move to leave.

"Colette, will you never tell me?"

"Yes," she replied unexpectedly, with a dancing light in her beautiful eyes.

"When?"

"When you restore to me what was in the pocket."

CHAPTER XVII

Jason never sought the Golden Fleece with more unwearying perseverance than John displayed in the pursuit of the lost article which Colette refused to describe. His calls of inquiry didn't mean merely putting the question politely and taking his departure after receiving an answer. It meant, in the case of Mrs. Hudgers, a martyr's test of patience in listening to the devious and manifold routes taken by her rheumatic pains; a rehearsal of the late lamented Hallie's idiosyncracies; the details of his last illness; his death; and his wearing of the surplice at the obsequies.

Throughout her harangue he preached patience unto himself and remembered that she was an old woman, desolate in her "lone lornness," so he counselled not, neither did he pray, but comforted her with the gentleness of voice and speech that won him a fond place in her memory for all time.

"No," she assured him decisively, as in departing he reminded her of his original question, "I didn't go fer to look in no pockit. I didn't suppose them things had pockits."

Then the scene shifted to Derry Phillips's studio, and this visit was fraught with more difficulties, for there was the case of Amarilly which must be approached delicately and with subtlety.

After stating his errand concisely and receiving assurance that the pocket had not been examined, but that the model should be interviewed by him, John still lingered.

"It's very kind in you to give employment to Amarilly, Mr. Phillips."

Derry shook his head.

"I am the one to be congratulated, Mr. Meredith. I really feel apologetic to Amarilly for accepting her services. They are so conscientiously and faithfully rendered that I feel she should be given a higher scope of work than she can find here. She is an honest, amusing little soul, and if by giving her employment I can encourage her desire to be industrious and earn something, I am very glad of the opportunity to do so."

99

This was a long and serious observation for the gay-hearted Derry to make, but he shrewdly fathomed the pastoral duty underlying the seemingly casual remark.

John's keen perception recognized the sincerity in the ring of the pleasant young voice, and he was quite won by the boyish directness. An instinctive confidence moved him to extend the right hand of trust and fellowship.

"You have been instructive as well as benevolent," he remarked smilingly. "Two of Amarilly's errors of speech have been eradicated."

The young Artist flushed in slight confusion, and then with a half-embarrassed laugh, he replied lightly: "Amarilly gave full measure of correction in return."

Responding to the nameless something in John that so insistently and irresistibly invited confidence, he related the little incident of the luncheon and her request in regard to temperate orders in the future.

"And I don't mean to say," he replied with winning frankness, "that it was merely the request of a little scrub-girl that has kept me temperate through two months of vacation and temptation, but the guileless suggestion was the spark that fired the flame of a dormant desire to change—certain conditions."

John again extended his hand, this time in a remorseful spirit of apology.

Derry partially understood.

"Amarilly has ardently interested friends," he observed whimsically. "There was one Vedder, a solemn young German, here to-day in my little maid's interest."

John's call upon the sable-hued preacher, Brother Washington, also demanded strategic approach. The question of pockets must be delicately handled lest any reflection be cast upon the integrity of the race, and their known penchant for pockets.

Brother Washington's sympathies were at once enlisted, however, when he scented a romance, for John became more confidential in this than in any of his prior visitations, in his desire to propitiate. But his search was fruitless here as elsewhere, and he went away convinced that Brother Washington had not tampered with the pocket.

He went on to the house of the Reverend James Woodville, who had performed the marriage ceremony at the nuptials of Mrs. Jimmels, née Hubbleston. In this instance also no pocket had been discovered in the garment, so John wended his discouraged way to the office of the Barlow Theatre.

Mr. Vedder was likewise surprised to learn that surplices possessed pockets.

The young rector's face brightened at the next name on his list—Pete

Noyes. Of course a boy and a pocket would not long remain unacquainted.

Again he was doomed to disappointment. Pete's dismay when he learned

that there had been an overlooked pocket was convincingly genuine.

"You see," he explained, "I wore it over my pants, of course, and I had the pockets in them, so I didn't look for no more."

Pete escorted the rector to the "Vawdyville," and by good fortune the clerical impersonator in the sketch was still on the board, though in a different act. He instantly and decidedly disclaimed all knowledge of a pocket.

"It's like that game," grinned Pete. "Button, button, who's got the button?"

"Yes," agreed John, with a sigh, "only in this case I fear I shall continue to be 'it.'"

The brakeman, when he came in from his run, was located and he joined in the blockade that was conspiring against John's future happiness.

The clothes-line thief was very sensitive on the subject, and felt greatly aggrieved that he should be accused of picking his own pocket, for he protested that he had "found" the garment. The fancied insinuation indeed was so strongly resented that John wondered if it might not be a proverbial case of "hit birds flutter."

101

Neither police nor court of justice had examined the pocket; nor had they been aware of the existence of one. The bishop could throw no light on the missing article, and this call ended the successless tour of investigation.

"It was truly a profitable investment for the Jenkins family," thought

John, "but a sorry one for me."

Having now wended his weary and unavailing way into all the places listed, John made his final report to Colette who remained adamant in her resolve.

"Of course some of those people did find it," she maintained. "It stands to reason they must have done so, and it is up to you now to find out which one of them is the guilty person."

"How can I find that out, Colette?"

"How? Anyhow!" she replied, her mien betraying great triumph at her powers of logic.

"It must be found!" she asserted with a distinct air of finality. "And until it is found—"

She stopped abruptly.

"Was it of value? No, I am not trying to find out what it was since you don't wish me to know, but if I knew its value, it might help me to decide who would be the most likely to have a motive for taking it. But my belief is that the article slipped from the pocket and is lost."

"It must be found then" she persisted obstinately.

John went home to ponder over his hopeless task. It remained for

Amarilly with her optimistic spirit to cheer him.

"It'll turn up some place whar you never looked fer it and when you ain't thinkin' nuthin' about it," she asserted believingly. "Lost things allers do."

Despite her philosophy she was greatly distressed over the disappearance of the mysterious article whose loss was keeping John so unhappy. She ransacked the house from the cellar to the Boarder's room, but found no trace of it.

"I wonder what it was," she mused.

"Mebby Miss King dreamt she put something in there, and when could she have done it anyhow? Mebby she give him a present, and he slipped it in there and fergot to take it out when he sent it to us. But then it would have come out in the wash. She don't seem to feel so bad as he does — jest sorter stubborn about it."

The members of the household were put through the third degree, but each declared his innocence in the matter.

"'Twas most likely Iry took it," said Cory, who found the baby a convenient loophole for any accusations, "and most likely he hez swallered it."

Gus persisted in his oft-repeated statement, that there was nothing in the pocket when it was hung up during quarantine. This assurance was conveyed to Colette by John, who hoped she might find solace in the thought that none of the renters could have had it, if this were true, but to his chagrin she found in his information an implied reflection on her veracity.

"Colette," he said whimsically, "only three persons connected with this affair have taken my remarks as personal, you, Brother Washington, and the thief."

With this remark John, despairing of his ability to fathom the mystery of the article or to follow the caprices of Colette, dropped the matter completely.

CHAPTER XVIII

At half past eight on the morning indicated, Amarilly's ring at the door of the studio was answered by Derry, whose face was covered with lather.

"Hello, Amarilly!" he exclaimed heartily, extending his hand in genial comradeship. "I am glad to see you again. Been pretty well through the summer? Well, come on into the butler's pantry, and see what you can do in a coffee way while I finish shaving."

Amarilly had been receiving instruction in domestic science, including table service, at the Guild school. Colette, interested in the studio work, had provided some minute muslin aprons and a little patch of linen for the head covering of the young waitress, advising her that she must wear them while serving breakfast. So when Derry emerged from his dressing-room, a trimly equipped little maid stood proudly and anxiously awaiting him.

"Why, bless your heart, Amarilly! I feel really domesticated. You look as natty as a new penny, and the little white cap is great on your hair. I see you have remembered how to fix it."

"Thank you, Mr. Derry, but please sit down while your coffee is hot."

"'Deed I will, and if it tastes as good as it smells, I shall raise your remuneration."

He pronounced the coffee delicious, the grapefruit fixed to his liking, the toast crisp, and the eggs boiled just to the right consistency.

"And have you had breakfast, Amarilly?"

"Yes, Mr. Derry, at half past five."

"Jiminy! you should be ready for another. Now talk to me while I eat. Tell me about your reverend friend who was so daffy on the subject of pockets. Has he located any yet?"

Amarilly looked troubled.

"Miss King said I wa'n't to talk to you while I was serving."

"Tell Miss King with Mr. Phillips' compliments that artists are not conventional, and that you and I are not in the relation to each other of master and maid. We are good friends, and quite en famille. You are such a fine cook, I think I shall have you serve me luncheon at one o'clock. Can you?" "Oh, yes; I should love to, Mr. Derry."

"I'll stock the larder, then. No; I can't be bothered, and I'd feel too much like a family man if I went about marketing. I'll give you carte blanche to order what you will."

"What's that, Mr. Derry?"

"Good! We mustn't neglect your education. I am glad you asked me. You might have always supposed it a breakfast-food."

He proceeded to explain elaborately what the words meant, and then asked her if she had remembered her previous lesson.

"Yes; ain't you—goin'—"

"Stop right there. Your next word to be eliminated is 'ain't.' You must say 'aren't' or 'isn't.' And you must remember to put 'g' on the end of every word ending in 'ing.' Don't let me hear you say 'goin', again, I'll teach you one new word every day now. You see the measure of a maid is her pure English."

Amarilly looked distressed.

"What's the matter, Amarilly? Don't you want to learn to speak properly?"

"Yes, I do, Mr. Derry; but Miss King—she don't want me to speak diff'rent. She likes to hear me talk ignorant, and she said she was afeard you'd make me brom—"

"Brom?" he repeated.

"There was some more to it, but I fergit."

"Bromidic," he said triumphantly, after an instant's pondering. "You can never under any circumstances be that, and I shall develop your imagination and artistic temperament at the same time. Miss King is selfish to wish to keep you from cultivating yourself for the purpose of furnishing her entertainment. By the way, I am to meet her to-night at a dinner, and I think we shall have a mutual subject for conversation. I must get to work, now. Clear away the dishes. And finish the rest of this toast and coffee. It would be wicked to waste it."

Amarilly substituted a work apron for the little white covering, and was soon engaged in "redding."

At eleven o'clock the place was in perfect order, and she went into the studio where Deny was at work.

"Shall I go get the things fer lunch?"

"Luncheon, if you please, Amarilly. I like that word better. It seems to mean daintier things. Here's a five-dollar bill. Get what you consider proper for a simple little home luncheon, you know. Nothing elaborate."

Amarilly, feeling but not betraying her utter inability to construct the menu for a "simple little home luncheon," walked despondently down the street.

"The Boarder," she reflected, "takes bread and meat and hard biled eggs when they ain't—aren't too high, and pie when we hev it."

Some vague instinct of the fitness of things warned her that this would not be a suitable repast for Derry. Then a light shone through her darkness.

"I'll telephone Miss Vail," she decided.

So she called up her teacher at the Guild, and explained the situation. She received full instructions, made her purchases, and went back to the studio.

At one o'clock she again garbed herself in cap and apron and called Derry to a luncheon which consisted of bouillon, chops, French peas, rolls, a salad, and black tea served with lemon.

"Amarilly," he announced solemnly, "you are surely the reincarnation of a chef. You are immediately promoted from housemaid to housekeeper with full charge over my cuisine, and your wages doubled."

"And that's going some for one day!" Amarilly gleefully announced to the family circle that night.

Her teacher, greatly interested and gratified at her pupil's ability to put her instruction to practical use and profit, made out on each Monday a menu for the entire week. She also gave her special coaching in setting table and serving, so Derry's domestic life became a thing of pride to himself and his coterie of artists. He gave little luncheons and studio teas in his apartments, Amarilly achieving great success in her double role of cook and waitress.

Her work was not only profitable financially, but it developed new tastes and tendencies. Every day there was the new word eagerly grasped and faithfully remembered. "Fer," "set," "spile," "orter," and the like were gradually entirely eliminated from her vocabulary. Unconsciously she acquired "atmosphere" from her environment. In her spare moments Amarilly read aloud to Derry, while he painted, he choosing the book at random from his library.

"I want to use you for a model this afternoon," he remarked one day as she was about to depart. "Braid your hair just as tight as you can, the way you had it the first day you came. Put on your high-necked, long- sleeved apron, and get it wet and soapy as it was that first day, and then come back to the studio with your scrubbing brush and pail."

Amarilly did as she was bidden with a reluctance which the artist, absorbed in his preparations for work, did not notice.

"Yes; that's fine," he said, glancing up as she came to him. "Now get down here on your knees by the—what kind of boards did you call them, Amarilly? Mopboards? Yes, that was it. Now try and put your whole mind on the memory of the horror you felt at the accumulation of dirt on that first day, and begin to scrub. Turn your head slightly toward me, tilted just a little—so—There, that's fine! Keep that position just as long and just as well as you possibly can."

Derry began to paint, mechanically at first, and then as he warmed to his subject and became interested in his conception, with rapidity and absorption.

"There!" he finally exclaimed, "you can rest now! This may be my chef-d'oeuvre, after all, Amarilly. Won't you be proud to be well hung in the Academy and have a group constantly before your picture. Why, what's the matter, child," springing to her side, "tears? I forgot it was your first experience in posing. Why didn't you tell me you were tired?"

"I wan't tired," she half sobbed.

"Well, what is it? Tell me."

"I'm afeerd you'll laugh at me."

"Not on your life! And your word for to-day, Amarilly, is afraid. Remember. Never afeerd."

"I'll remember," promised Amarilly meekly, as she wiped her dewy eyes.

"Now tell me directly, what is the matter."

"It'll be such a humbly picture with my hair that way. I'd ought to look my best. I'd rather you'd paint me waiting on your table."

"But a waitress is such a trite subject. It would be what your friend, I mean, our friend, Miss King, calls bromidic. An artist, a real artist, with a soul, Amarilly, doesn't look for pretty subjects. It's the truth that he seeks. To paint things as they are is what he aims to do. A little scrub-girl appeals to the artistic temperament more than a little waitress, don't you think? But only you, Amarilly, could look the part of the Little Scrub-Girl as you did. And it would be incongruous— remember the word, please, Amarilly, in-con-gru-ous—to paint her with stylishly dressed hair. You posed so easily, so perfectly, and your expression was so precisely the one I wanted, and your patience in keeping the pose was so wonderful, that I thought you had really caught the spirit of the thing, and were anxious to help me achieve my really great picture."

"I have—I will pose for you as long as you wish," she cried penitently, "and I will braid my hair on wire, and then it will stand out better."

"Good! You are a dear, amenable little girl. To-morrow afternoon we will resume. Here, let me loosen your braids. Goodness, what thick strands!"

She stood by the open window, and the trembling, marginal lights of a setting sun sent gleams and glints of gold through her loosened hair which fell like a flaming veil about her.

"Amarilly," exclaimed Derry rapturously, "I never saw anything quite so beautiful. Some day I'll paint you, not as a scrub-girl nor as a waitress, but as Sunset. You shall stand at this window with your hair as it is now, and you'll outshine the glory of descending Sol himself. I will get a filmy, white dress for you to pose in and present it to you afterward. And as you half turn your head toward the window, you must have a dreamy, reflective expression! You must think of something sad, something that might have been a tragedy but for some mitigating—but there, you don't know what I am talking about!"

"Yes, I do, Mr. Derry. I know what you mean, even if I didn't ketch—"

"Catch, Amarilly; not ketch."

"But my word for to-day is 'afraid,'" she said stubbornly. "I wasn't to have but one word a day. I'll say 'ketch' until to-morrow."

"Oh, Amarilly, such system as you have! You are right though; but tell me what it was I meant." "You mean I am to think of something awful that would have been more awful but for something nice that happened. I'll think of the day last summer when we couldn't pay the rent. That was sad until the bishop came along and things got brighter."

"Exactly. You have the temperament, Amarilly, but you should have written to your twin brother in such a dilemma. It's late now, or it will be when you get home. I am going to walk with you."

"No; I am not afraid."

"It makes no difference; I am going with you. To think that, intimate friends as we are, I have never seen your home, your numerous brothers, and the Boarder. I am going to spend the evening with you."

"Oh, no!" she protested, appalled at the prospect. "You mustn't."

"Why, Amarilly, how inhospitable you are! I thought you would be pleased."

"I guess you couldn't stand for it."

"Stand for what, Amarilly?"

"Why, you see, I am not ashamed of it, but it's so diff'rent from what you're used to, and you wouldn't like it, and I'd feel uncomfortable like with you

there." "Why, Amarilly!" A really pained look came into his boyish eyes. "I thought we were friends. And you let Miss King and your minister come —
"

"But you see," argued Amarilly, "it's diff'rent with them. A minister has to go everywhere, and he's used to seeing all kinds of houses; and then Miss King, she's a sort of a — settlement worker."

"I see," said Derry. "But, Amarilly, to be a true artist, or a writer, one must see all sorts and conditions of life. But I am not coming for that. I am coming because I like you and want to meet your family."

"Well," agreed Amarilly, resigned, but playing her last trump, "you haven't had your dinner yet."

"We had a very late luncheon, if you remember, and I am invited to a supper after the theatre to-night, so I am not dining."

Amarilly did not respond to his light flow of chatter on the way home. She halted on the threshold of her home, and looked at him with despair in her honest young eyes.

"Our house hasn't got any insides or any stairs even. Just a ladder."

"Good! I knew you wouldn't — that you couldn't have a house like anyone's else. It sounds interesting and artistic. Open your door to me, Amarilly."

Slowly she opened the door, and drew a sigh of relief. The big room was "tidied" ("redded" having been censored by Derry some time ago) and a very peaceful, homelike atmosphere prevailed. The Boarder, being an amateur carpenter, had made a very long table about which were grouped the entire family. Her mother was darning socks; the Boarder, reading the paper preliminary to his evening call on Lily Rose; the boys, busy with books and games; Cory, rocking her doll to sleep.

Their entrance made quite a little commotion. There was a scattering of boys from the table until Derry called "Halt" in stentorian tones. "If there's any gap in the circle, I shall go."

Then he joined the group, and described to the boys a prize-fight so graphically that their eyes fastened on him with the gaze of one witnessing the event itself. He praised Amarilly to the mother, gave Cory a "tin penny" which she at once recognized as a silver quarter, and talked politics so eloquently with the Boarder that for once he was loath to leave when the hour of seven-thirty arrived.

"You've gotter go now," reminded Cory sternly. "You see," turning to Derry. "he's gotter go and spend his ev'nin' with Lily Rose. She's his gal."

"Oh! Well, why not bring her here to spend the evening?" suggested Derry. "Then you'll have an excuse for two nice walks and an evening thrown in."

"That's a fine, idee!" acknowledged the Boarder with a sheepish grin.

He at once set out on his quest accompanied by Bobby, whom Derry had dispatched to the corner grocery for a supply of candy and peanuts.

The Boarder and Lily Rose came in laden with refreshments. The Boarder bore a jug of cider "right on the turn," he declared, "so it stings your throat agoin' down."

Lily Rose had brought a bag of sugared doughnuts which she had made that afternoon (a half holiday) in her landlady's kitchen.

When Mrs. Jenkins learned from Amarilly that Derry and she had had nothing to eat since half past one, she brought forth a pan of beans and a pumpkin pie, and they had a genuine New England supper. The Boarder recited thrilling tales of railroad wrecks. Derry listened to a solo by Bud, whose wild-honeyed voice was entrancing to the young artist. Altogether they were a jolly little party, Lily Rose saying little, but looking and listening with animated eyes. Mrs. Jenkins declared afterwards that it was the time of her life.

"Amarilly," said Derry, as he was taking leave, "I wouldn't have missed this evening for any other engagement I might have made."

"That's because it was something new to you," said Amarilly sagely. "You wouldn't like it for keeps."

CHAPTER XIX

When Cory secured a place as dish-wiper at a new boarding-house near, and Gus realized that he and Iry alone were dependent upon the others for their keep, shame seared his young soul. He had vainly tried to secure steady employment, but had succeeded only in getting occasional odd jobs. He had a distinct leaning towards an agricultural life and coveted the care of cows.

"The grocer has sold his'n," he lugubriously lamented; "thar ain't no one else as wants a caretaker for their critters around here."

After a long rumination on the discouraging problem of his future, he sought his confessor, the corner grocer.

"I'm too big to peddle papers or be runnin' about with telergrafs," he declared. "I'd orter be goin' into business on my own account. I ain't goin' ter be allers workin' fer other folks."

"Well, you'll have to wait a while before you can work for yourself," counselled his confidant. "You are young yet."

"This is a hurry-up age," was the sagacious assertion, "and ef you air agoin' to git any-whar, you've got ter go by wire instead of by mail, and you can't start too soon."

"You can't start nothing without capital," argued the grocer conservatively.

"Oh," admitted the young financier, "a little capital mebby. I've got a dollar I've saved up from odd jobs."

"What line was you thinking of taking up?"

"I'm going into the dairy business. Thar's money in milk and butter, and it's nice, clean work."

"The dairy business on one dollar! How many cows and wagons and horses was you figuring on buying with your dollar?"

"Don't git funny," warned Gus impatiently. "Some day I'll hev a farm of my own and a city office, but I'll begin on one cow in our back lot and peddle milk to the neighbors."

"That wouldn't be a bad beginning, but I reckon you'll find the start will cost you more than a dollar. You can't get a cow at that figure."

"Then I'll start with a calf."

"Well, I guess calves cost more than a dollar."

"Say, you've got that dollar on the brain, I guess," retorted the lad with the easy familiarity that betokened long acquaintance with the lounging barrels and boxes of the corner grocery. "I bet it'll build a shed in our back yard. Thar's the lumber out of our shed that blowed down, and the Boarder can build purty near anything."

"But how are you going to buy a cow?" persisted his inquisitor.

"I ain't got that fer yet," admitted the young dairyman.

"Your dollar'll buy more than the nails for your cow-house. You can put the balance into feed," said the grocer, with an eye to his own trade.

He wanted to add that it wouldn't cost much to feed an imaginary critter, but he was a little fearful of the temper back of the lad's hair, which was the same hue as Amarilly's.

"That's a good idea. Well, the shed starts to-morrow, and of course you won't say nothin' about it."

"Trust me for not talking in this neighborhood. It ain't safe even to think. First you know your thoughts are being megaphoned down the street."

Gus consulted the Boarder who instantly and obligingly began the erection of a building in the farthest corner of the Jenkins's domain. This structure was a source of mystery and excitement to the neighbors.

"What on airth do you suppose them Jenkinses air aputtin' up now? Mebby it's a wash-house for the surpluses," speculated Mrs. Huce.

"It can't be they air agoin' to keep a hoss!" ejaculated Mrs. Wint.

"You never kin tell nuthin' about them Jenkinses. They're so sort of secretin' like," lamented Mrs. Hudgers.

The Jenkins family were fully as ignorant as were their neighbors of the nature of the contemplated occupant of the new edifice commonly referred to as the "cow-house," The Boarder put up a very substantial shed with a four-paned window and a door that locked though not very securely. The grocer had on hand a small quantity of green paint which he donated to the cause of the coming cow.

"Thar ain't enough to more'n paint two sides of it," criticized Gus, "so

I'll paint the front and west sides."

"Thar's a can of yaller paint out in the woodshed," informed Mrs.

Jenkins. "You can paint the other two sides with that."

Then the Boarder made a suggestion:

"If I was you, I'd paint a strip of yaller and then one of green.

That'll even it up and make it fancy-like."

Amarilly protested against this combination of colors so repellent to artistic eyes, but the family all agreed that it "would be perfickly swell," so she withdrew her opposition and confided her grievance to Derry's sympathizing, shuddering ears.

Gus proceeded to bicolor the shed in stripes which gave the new building a bedizened and bilious effect that delighted Colette, who revelled in the annals of her protegés.

Each member of the Jenkins family had a plan for utilising this fine domicile, as there seemed to be a general feeling of skepticism regarding the ability of Gus to produce a cow in the flesh. This sentiment, however, was not openly expressed, as the lad was found to be decidedly sensitive and touchy on the subject.

"Mebby a cow'll jest walk right into the back yard and make herself to hum in the new shed," prognosticated Mrs. Jenkins optimistically. "It's such a beautiful place. I'll bet there is cows as would ef they knowed about it."

"I perpose," suggested Flamingus patronizingly, "that we start a cow fund and all chip in and help Gus out."

"Sure thing!" declared the generous Amarilly. "He can have all my savings. We ought to all help Gus get a start."

"I'm in," cried Bobby.

"You kin hev all you want from me, Gus," offered Bud.

Firmly and disdainfully Gus rejected all these offers and suggestions.

"Thar ain't agoin' to be no pardner business about this," he announced. "The cow won't come till she's mine—all mine—and when she does, I'm agoin' to pay the Boarder for his work."

"If he wants to be so all-fired smart, we won't help him git no cow," declared Flamingus, "and the shed kin be used for a summer kitchen arter all."

This use of the new building had been the fondest dream of Mrs. Jenkins, who deemed it an ideal place in which to keep her tubs, mops, boiler, and wringer. Milt had designs upon it for a boy's reading-room and club; Flamingus coveted a gymnasium. Bobby, Bud, Cory, and Iry had already appropriated it as a playhouse.

Amarilly openly and ably defended Gus and his cherished, illusory plan. Of all her brothers, he was the one to whom her heart most inclined. For Bud she possibly had a more tender, maternal feeling on account of his being so delicate. She paid homage to the good points of Flamingus, but he was too cut and dried, "bromidic," she classified him, for Derry had carefully explained the etymology of the word. Milt was honest, but selfish and "near." Bobby was disposed to be fresh, but Gus was just such a boy as Amarilly herself would have been, reincarnated. He was practical, industrious, thrifty, and shrewd, and yet possessed of the imagination and optimism of his sister. She called him aside one day for a private consultation.

"Say, Gus, your scheme's all right. Go ahead and get your cow. I'll let you have my savings, and the other boys needn't know. You can pay me when you get ready to."

"That's bully in you, Amarilly, but I'm agoin' to see this thing through alone and start in without no help front no one," firmly refused Gus, and his sturdy little sister could but admire him for his independence.

He locked up his new possession very carefully, putting the key in his pocket every morning before going to the business precincts to pick up a job. The children, however, were not dispossessed by this precaution, finding ingress and egress through the window. Gus most opportunely secured a week's job driving a delivery-wagon, and he instantly invested his wages in the provisioning of the cow quarters.

"The feed'll git stale by the time the cow comes," objected Milt.

"Mebby it's fer bait to ketch a critter with," offered Bobby.

After all, it was the miracle predicted by Mrs. Jenkins that came to pass and delivered the cow. Early one morning, when Gus went as usual with fond pride to view his sole asset, he found installed therein a young, corpulent cow, bland and Texas-horned, busily engaged in partaking of the proceeds of Gus's last week's wages. She turned inquiring, meditative eyes toward the delighted lad, who promptly locked the door and rushed into the house to inform the family of the new arrival.

"She's lost or strayed, but not stolen," said Amarilly.

"Bobby, you put an ad in that paper you deliver at once," commanded Mrs. Jenkins. "Some poor people air feelin' bad over the loss of their cow."

It was considered only fair that the cow should pay for her meal. She was overstocked with milk, and graciously and gratefully yielded to Gus's efforts to relieve her of her load. The children were each given a taste of the warm milk, and then the little dairyman started right in for business. The milkman had not yet made his morning rounds, and the neighbors were so anxious to cross-examine Gus that they were more than willing to patronize him. Excitement prevailed when it was learned that the Jenkins family had a cow, and the lad's ingenuity in dodging questions was severely taxed. He avoided direct replies, but finally admitted that it was "one they was keepin' fer some folks."

A week went by, with no claim filed for the animal that had come so mysteriously and seemed so perfectly at home. Gus established a permanent milk route in the immediate neighborhood, and with his ability once more to "bring in" came the restoration of his self-respect.

"It's funny we don't git no answer to that ad," mused Mrs. Jenkins perplexedly. "How many times did you run it, Bobby?"

For a moment silence, deep, profound, and charged with expectancy prevailed. Then like a bomb came Bobby's reply:

"I ain't put it in at all."

Everybody was vociferous in condemnation, but Bobby, unabashed, held his ground, and logically defended his action.

"I got the news-agent to look in the 'losts' every night, and thar want nothin' about no cow. 'Twas up to them as lost it to advertise instead of us. If they didn't want her bad enough to run an ad, they couldn't hev missed her very much."

"That's so," agreed the Boarder, convinced by Bobby's able argument.

"Most likely she doesn't belong to any one," was Amarilly's theory. "She just came to stay a while, and then she'll go away again."

"She won't git no chanst to 'scape, unless she kin go out the way the chillern does," laughed Mrs. Jenkins.

One day the Boarder brought home some information that seemed to throw light on the subject.

"One of the railroad hands told me that a big train of cattle was sidetracked up this way somewhar the same night the cow come here. The whole keerload got loose, but they ketched them all, or thought they did. Mebby they didn't miss this ere one, or else they couldn't wait to look her up. Their train pulled out as soon as they rounded up the bunch."

"I guess the cow-house looked to her like it was a freight car," observed Milt, "and she thought she hed got back where she belonged."

The cow, meanwhile, quietly chewed her cud, and continued to endear herself to the hearts of all the Jenkins family save Cory. Every time Bobby spoke her name he called to her, "Co, boss! Co, boss," just as Gus did when he greeted the cow.

As for the little dairyman himself, he gave his charge the best of care. He took her for a little outing every day to a near-by lot where she could graze, being careful to keep a stout rope attached to her, although they walked to and from the recreation ground side by side. Derry painted a little picture of the pair as he saw them returning from a jaunt. Gus's arm was lovingly thrown around the neck of the gentle creature, and her Texas horns were adorned with a wreath of brown-eyed Susans woven by Cory.

It remained for Mrs. Jenkins to christen the creature.

"'Cowslip,'" she declared triumphantly, "'cause she just slipped in."

CHAPTER XX

Amarilly's pace in learning English from Derry during the following winter was only excelled by her proficiency in mathematics. "Figgerin'" the Boarder declared to be his long suit, and his young pupil worked every example in Flamingus's arithmetic, and employed her leisure moments in solving imaginary problems. Then came an evening when she put her knowledge to practical use and application. She had been working absorbedly with pencil and paper for some time when she looked up from her sheet of figures with a flushed race and a Q.E.D. written in each shining eye.

"Say!" she announced to the family who were gathered about the long table.

Instantly they were all attention, for they always looked to Amarilly for something startling in the way of bulletins.

"I've been setting down and adding up what we all bring in each week.

Ma's washings, the Boarder's board, my studio work, Flamingus' and

Milt's wages, Gus's cow, Bud's singing, Co's dish-washing, and Bobby's

papers. What do you suppose it all amounts to?"

She allowed a few seconds of tragic silence to ensue before she gave the electrifying total.

"Land sakes! Who'd 'a thought it!" exclaimed Mrs. Jenkins.

"We'd orter hev ice-cream and pie every day," reproached Cory.

"It would be reckoned a purty big salary if one man got it all," speculated the Boarder.

"We are rich!" exclaimed Bobby decisively.

"I'll tell you what we'll do," pursued Amarilly. "We must start a syndicate."

"What's that, a show?" demanded Flamingus.

"No; I heard the artists down to the studio talking about it, and Mr. Derry explained it. He said when a lot of folks put their cash on hand together in one pile, they can buy something big and do more than as if they spent it separate."

"Well, I ain't a goin' to put my money in with Co's," said Milt sarcastically. "Wouldn't be much profit for me in that."

"You don't catch on," replied Amarilly. "If you should put in one dollar, and Co should put in ten cents, at the end of a certain time, you'd draw out ten dollars and Co would only draw out one. See?"

"I do," said the practical Gus.

"Well, now let's put our money into something and all own it together, each one's share according to what we put in. Let's buy this house!"

They all stared in amazement.

"Buy a house! You are sure crazy, Amarilly!" exclaimed Milt.

"We could buy it cheap," continued Amarilly unabashed. "I heard the grocer saying yesterday that property around here was at a low figure now. We could put our savings together and make a payment down, and instead of paying rent let it go on the balance each month. Before we knew it we'd own the house, and the deed could be made out to show how much of it each one owned."

"I choose the pantry!" cried Cory.

"I guess if you could buy a window-pane with what you've got, you'd do well," observed Milt in a withering tone.

"That's a splendid idee, Amarilly!" declared the Boarder enthusiastically. "I don't know what better investment you could make."

"It would be fine," sighed Mrs. Jenkins, "to own your own place and feel that no one could turn you out."

"You've got a great head, Amarilly," complimented Gus.

"We could borrow on the house if we ever got hard up, or the fever struck us again," said Flamingus.

"Well," proposed Amarilly, the ever-ready, "let's get right at it. I'll set down our names, and when I call the roll, tell me how much you've saved and will put in the house."

There was a general rush for bank-books, for ever since the preceding fall, the six oldest children had paid their board, clothed themselves, and saved the balance of their earnings.

From her washings, the revenue from the board of the children and Boarder, Mrs. Jenkins had paid the rent and the household expenses. By thrifty management she had also acquired a bank account herself.

"Ma!" called Amarilly expectantly.

There had been much urging on the part of

Deny in his zeal for language reform to induce his young pupil to say "mother," but in this sole instance Amarilly had refused to take his will for law.

"She's always been 'ma' to me, and she always will be," declared Amarilly emphatically. "If I were to call her anything else I'd feel as if I had lost her — as if she didn't belong to me."

Ma triumphantly announced: "Forty-seven dollars and fifty-one cents."

"A fine starter," commended Amarilly, "Flamingus?"

"Forty dollars," he announced with pride.

"Milt?" Amarilly called his name in faint voice. He was the only tight-tendencied member of the household, and she feared he might decline to give. But Milt was envious and emulative.

"Forty-two dollars and sixty-nine cents," he declared in a voice rendered triumphant by the fact of his having beaten Flam.

Amarilly drew a sigh of relief.

"It's going to add up fine, now. Guess I'll take my own account next. I haven't got as much as you boys, though." "Shouldn't think you would have," said Gus sympathizingly. "You don't earn so much, and yet you pay ma as much, and don't take out nuthin' fer your noon meal. And you give Co things."

"I've earned quite a bit," replied Amarilly cheerfully. "Besides what Mr. Derry gives me, there's what I've had from odd jobs like letting the artists paint my hair, and taking care of Mrs. Wick's baby afternoons when she goes to card parties. I've got thirty dollars to put in. Gus?"

"Thirty-five dollars," he replied in a pleased tone.

"Bud?"

They all looked expectantly. Bud received ten dollars each Sunday now, and he had been singing at concerts, organ recitals, and entertainments all winter. On account of these latter engagements, he had been obliged to expend a considerable amount in clothes suitable to the occasion. When Bud donned his "evening clothes," which consisted of black silk hose, patent leather pumps, black velvet suit with Irish crochet collar and cuffs, purchased under the direction of Mr. Derry, Amarilly always felt uncomfortable.

"Don't seem fair to Bobby when they're so near twins," she thought.

One day, however, she overheard Bud sweetly offer to buy his near half a similar outfit. Amarilly listened eagerly for Bobby's answer which brought a sigh of relief.

"I wouldn't wear one of them rigs on a bet," he had scoffingly answered.

"One hundred and twenty-five dollars," Bud now replied modestly.

"Gee! you take the cake!" said Bobby.

Amarilly was sorry that she had to call Bobby's name next. But Bobby had a surprise in store for them all.

"Forty-eight dollars!" he cried gleefully, giving Flam, Milt and Gus exultant glances, "Beat the hull of ye, except Bud!"

"How in the world did you ever do it on paper routes?" asked Amarilly wonderingly.

Bobby winked at his mother.

"Shall we tell our secret?" he asked. "You tell, Ma."

"You see," she explained, "when the clo'es are bilin' arter you hev all gone to work and to school, I've made twenty little pies and when Bobby got out of school, he'd come hum and git 'em and take 'em up to the High School. The girls bought 'em at five cents apiece. The stuff to make 'em cost about two cents a pie."

"And Bobby got all the profit!" expostulated Milt indignantly.

"Bobby paid me by taking the clo'es offen the line and bringin' them in every night, and fetchin' the water," she replied chidingly. "We was goin' to keep it a secret till he got enough to buy a pony."

"But I'd ruther buy a house," said Bobby.

"I ain't got enough to come in no snidikit," sobbed Co. "I ain't saved much."

"That's because you spend all you earn on candy," rebuked Milt.

"I ain't nuther. I bought me some rubbers and Iry some playthings."

"How much have you got, Co?" asked Amarilly gently.

"Two dollars and ninety-seven cents," she said, weeping profusely.

"I think that's pretty good for a little girl," said Amarilly. "All you strapping boys ought to chip in out of your cash on hand what isn't in the bank and give her some so she could be in on it. Here is fifty cents from me, Co."

"I'll give you fifty, Co," said her mother.

"Me, too," said Flamingus.

The other boys followed with equal contributions, Bud generously donating a five-dollar bill he had received that day for a solo at a musicale given by Miss Lyte.

"Here's fifty cents from me," said the Boarder, who had remained very thoughtful during this transaction.

"Eleven dollars and forty-seven cents for Co," announced Amarilly.

The little girl's eyes shone through her tears.

"Seems too bad that Iry is the only one left out," said Mrs. Jenkins.

"When he gits old enough to work, he can come in," said Milt. "Add her up, Amarilly."

"Three hundred and sixty-nine dollars and sixty-seven cents!" almost screamed Amarilly.

"Gee!" chorused the boys.

"Purty near buy the old shack," said Flamingus.

"Our landlord," said Amarilly sagaciously, "is a shark, and he'll try to get the best of us. I am going to get Mr. Vedder to do the business for us, and he'll get the deed in all our names."

"Put in Iry's too," pleaded Mrs. Jenkins solicitous for her Benjamin.

"I'll put it to vote," said parliamentary Amarilly. "Who's for Iry?"

"Me, me, me," came from all, though Milt's response was reluctant.

"I will see Mr. Vedder to-morrow, so we can begin to let the rent apply right off," said Amarilly.

"We'll take more pride in keeping it fixed up now," remarked Flamingus.

"I'll mend the windowpanes and the door hinges."

"And I'll build some stairs and put up a partition or two," promised the Boarder.

"I'll paint it," said Gus, proud of his former work in this direction.

Amarilly secretly resolved to select the color.

"I'll make curtains and rag rugs and sofa pillows," she observed.

"And I'll buy some cheers and a hangin' lamp," said Mrs. Jenkins. "Don't all this talk make you want to housekeep?" she asked with a knowing glance in the Boarder's direction.

He shook his head thoughtfully, but when the boys and Cory had gone to bed, he unfolded a proposition that he had been evolving during their financial discussion, and which now found overwhelming favor and enthusiasm with his hearers.

The next day Amarilly called upon Mr. Vedder at the theatre.

"He's got more sound business to him than Mr. Derry or Mr. St. John," she shrewdly decided.

"When she told him her plan and showed him her figures, he most heartily approved.

"The house, of course, isn't worth anything," he said, "but land down that way is a good investment. Who is your, landlord?"

She gave him the name and address.

"I am glad you came to me, Amarilly, instead of to your newer friends."

"Oh, you know more about it than they do," she replied, "and besides, some way I wouldn't feel as if I were bothering you."

"Not a bit of bother, Amarilly, and I hope you will always feel that way."

The ticket-seller was prompt, thorough, and shrewd in the matter. He had a friend in the real estate business, who appraised the property for him, and he proved most diplomatic in his dealing with the surprised landlord, who fortunately chanced to be in dire need of some ready cash. In an incredibly short space of time the bargain was closed.

The Jenkins family including the Boarder and Iry left the house one noon, each bearing a red bank-book. To the onlookers in the neighborhood, this Armada was all-impressive.

"Looks like a run on the bank," said the Boarder facetiously, as they all trooped up the steps to the big stone building.

The payment was made, and the deeds drawn in the names of all the family, but to the list was also added the name of the Boarder.

CHAPTER XXI

"I don't see," observed Colette, on learning of the existence and development of the syndicate, "why the Boarder is in on it. I thought he was going to have a Lily Rose garden all his own."

"We thought so, too," replied Amarilly. "He's been saving up to get married, and he's got a raise now, so the day is set for some time in June; but he told us the night we were first planning to buy the house that he wanted to be one of the syndicate. You see Lily Rose works — I mean she overworks — in a factory, and so the Boarder — you know he is awful gentle-like to her — says that she mustn't keep house or do anything but real light work after this. He has an interest in the house now, and he is going to build on a sort of an annex with a sitting-room and a bedroom and furnish it up fine, and when they are married, they are going to live there and take their meals with us. And they want Mr. St. John to marry them, and they want you to come. And Mr. Derry is coming. He asked to be invited."

For once Colette did not laugh at the chronicles of the Jenkins family.

A very tender look came into her flashing eyes.

"That is very sweet in him — in the Boarder — to feel that way and to be so tender with Lily Rose. She ought to be very happy with a love and protection like that awaiting her."

"Yes," assented Amarilly; "it must be very nice to feel like that, and Mr. Derry says he really believes that it is only with poor folks like us and the Boarder and Lily Rose that love runs smooth."

"Then," said Colette musingly, "I wish I were poor — like you and the

Boarder and Lily Rose!"

Amarilly secretly divined that this was merely a thought spoken aloud, so she made no comment. She had pondered a great deal over the attitude of her two friends towards each other. The only place she ever encountered them together was at church and to her observing eyes it was quite apparent that there was a restraint in their bearing. Amarilly remained so preoccupied with her thoughts that Colette, looking at her searchingly, became curious as to the cause.

"Amarilly," she commanded, "tell me what you were thinking of just now — I mean since I spoke last. I shall know by; your eyes if you don't tell me exactly."

"Mr. Derry says my eyes will always give me away," evaded Amarilly.

"Of course they will. You can never be a flirt, Amarilly."

"I don't want to," she replied indignantly.

Colette laughed.

"Well, tell me what you were thinking about?"

"I was wondering if Mr. St. John wasn't trying any more to find that thing you lost in the surplice pocket."

"Oh, Amarilly, has Mr. Phillips censored that word, too? I was in hopes he would never hear you say 'surplus,' so he could not correct you."

"I told him you didn't want me to speak correctly," said Amarilly a little resentfully.

"You did!" cried Colette, looking rather abashed. "And what did he say?"

"He said it was selfish in you to think more of your amusement than of my improvement."

Colette colored and was silent a moment.

"He's right, Amarilly," she said impulsively. "I am selfish to everyone. All I have ever cared for is to be entertained and made to laugh. I have been as selfish to St. John as I have to you and — I'll tell you a secret, Amarilly, because I know that I can trust you. I've gone just a little bit too far with St. John. I told him he needn't ever come to see me again until he found what was in the pocket of the surplice, and he took me at my word."

"He did all he could to find it," said Amarilly, immediately on the defence for the rector.

"I know he did, but you see before this I've always had everything I've asked for, even impossible things, and I didn't want to have him fail me. I have been selfish and exacting with him, and I think he realizes it now."

"Well, when you're in the wrong, all you've got to do is to say so."

"That isn't easy, Amarilly."

"But it's right."

"Oh, Amarilly, you're like a man with your right and your wrong!"

"But you would make yourself happy, too, if you told him you knew it wasn't up to him any more to find that."

"I'd rather be unhappy and stick to what I said. I must have my own way, Amarilly."

"Well," said Amarilly, abandoning an apparently hopeless subject, "I came to ask you to do me — us — the Boarder and Lily Rose, I mean, a favor."

"What is it, Amarilly?"

"Why, as I said, they want Mr. St. John to marry them, and they're afraid he won't want to because he — well — because he isn't their kind, you know, and he has such a fashionable church."

"And you don't know St. John better than that?"

"Why, yes; of course I do, but they don't know him at all, you know. And the Boarder is real shy, anyhow. And so I told him I'd ask you to ask him."

"Why don't you ask him?"

"I think it would please him so to have you ask. He likes to have you take interest in others."

"Amarilly, you are a regular little Sherlock! Well, yes, I will," promised Colette, secretly glad of this opportunity for friendly converse with John once more, "but if the — Annex has to be built first, there's no hurry."

"Yes, there is. The Boarder wants everything settled now, so they can be looking forward to it."

"Very well, Amarilly. I'll see him to-morrow night. Will that do?"

"Oh, yes; thank you, Miss King."

"Tell me more about the wedding plans. Are you to be bridesmaid?"

"She isn't going to have one. It won't be a stylish wedding, you know. Just quiet—like one of our neighborhood evenings. Only when I told Mr. Derry about it, he said he should come up that afternoon and trim the house up with greens, and that he should come to see them married."

"And I shall furnish the flowers and the bride's bouquet. Let me see, I think lilies of the valley and pink roses would suit Lily Rose, don't you?"

"They will be beautiful," said Amarilly, beaming. "And we are going to have a real swell meal. I have learned to make salads and ices, and then we'll have coffee and sandwiches and bride's cake beside."

"Some one has to give the bride away, you know, Amarilly, in Episcopal weddings."

"I know it. But poor Lily Rose has no one that belongs to her. Her relations are all dead. That's another reason why the Boarder is so nice to her. So ma is going to give her away. We're going to ask the neighbors and you and Mr. Derry and Mr. Cotter, of course. He's the brakeman friend of the Boarder."

"And are the Boarder and Lily Rose going away?"

"Yes; the Boarder can get a pass to Niagara Falls. They are going to stay there a week. Lily Rose has never been on the cars. And they are going to ride to the train in a hack."

"Why, it's going to be quite an affair," said Colette enthusiastically. "We'll throw an old shoe and some rice after them. And will she be married in white?"

Amarilly's face fell.

"I am afraid she can't afford a wedding dress. She's got to get a travelling suit and hat and gloves and shoes, and with other things it will take all she has saved. She'd like a white dress and a veil and get her picture taken in it to hang up by the side of the Boarder's in the surplice. And that makes me think, we want you to ask Mr. St. John if he will wear our surplice instead of bringing one of his. We'll do it up nice before the wedding."

"Oh, that prophetic surplice!" groaned Colette. "It's yesterday, to-day and forever; I wish something would happen to it, Amarilly. I hate that surplice!"

"I'm sorry, Miss King, but we all love it. And you see it means a good deal to Lily Rose; because she has looked at its photograph so long."

"Very well, Amarilly. I yield. St. John shall wear his surplice once more, and when he does—"

A sudden thought illumined her face. "I believe I will tell him—"

Amarilly deemed it a fitting time to depart, and she hastened to assure

Lily Rose that it was "all right."

"Miss King will speak to Mr. St. John about marrying you, and she will ask him to wear our surplice. She's going to send you flowers—lilies of the valley and roses. It all would be perfect, Lily Rose, if only you had a white dress!"

Lily Rose smiled sweetly, and told Amarilly she was glad to be married in any dress, and that she should not miss the "reg'ler weddin' fixin's" nearly as much as Amarilly would mind her not having them. When Amarilly set her head and heart on anything, however, it was sure to be accomplished. It was a puzzling problem to equip Lily Rose in the conventional bridal white vestments, for the bride-to-be was very proud and independent and wouldn't hearken to Amarilly's plea to be allowed to contribute toward a new dress.

"We're under obligations to him, you know," argued Amarilly "and I'd like to help him by helping you."

Lily Rose was strong of will despite her sweet smile.

Deep down in her heart Amarilly, throughout all her scheming, knew there was a way, but she chose to ignore it until the insistent small voice spoke louder and louder. With a sigh of renunciation she yielded to the inevitable and again sought Lily Rose.

"I've thought out a way to the white dress," she announced.

Lily Rose's eyes sparkled for a moment, and their light died out.

"Yes, there's really a way," persisted Amarilly, answering the unspoken denial. "You said you could squeeze out slippers and stockings, didn't you?"

"Yes," she admitted.

"Well, there's your new white dress skirt, and for a waist there is my lovely lace waist that I told you about — the one Miss King gave me."

"Your weddin' waist! No, Amarilly. It's like you to offer, but I couldn't take it from you."

"No, I'm not giving it to you. Just lending it to you for your wedding. You couldn't hurt it any wearing it two hours. Then I'll lay it by again till I'm married. And I'll like wearing it all the more because you wore it to your wedding. Come over some day and we'll try it on. Then Miss King is going to give you the bouquet, and for a veil —"

"Oh, the veil! Amarilly, I would love a veil!" Lily Rose cried wistfully.

"Well, I've got one spoken for. You see, Mrs. Jimmels has been married so many different ways, I felt sure she must have worn a veil at one of her weddings, and seeing she had been married so many times, I thought she couldn't have any special feeling about any one of them, so I asked her if she wouldn't lend hers to you, and she's glad to have it put to use again. You'll look just perfectly swell, Lily Rose. And she's going to give you a pair of white gloves that she had when she was slim-like."

The little renunciator went home feeling amply rewarded by the look of shining content in the blue eyes of Lily Rose.

The next night Colette in accordance with her promise to Amarilly summoned John to council. It was not easy to bridge the distance which had been steadily increasing with the months that had rolled by since the surplice dénouement, and Colette, formerly supreme in her sway, was perceptibly timid in making the advance. After writing and tearing up several notes she called him up by telephone and asked him in a consciously casual tone if he could find it convenient to call that evening with reference to a little matter pertaining to their mutual charge, the Jenkinses.

The grave voice in which he accepted the invitation was tinged with pleasure.

When he came Colette, fearful lest he should misinterpret her action in making this overture, plunged at once into the subject.

"I promised Amarilly I would see you and ask you for something in her friends' behalf."

"Then it is to Amarilly I am indebted for this call," he remarked whimsically.

"It's about the Boarder," she continued, gaining ease at the softening of his brown eyes. "You know he is to be married to Lily Rose, the girl we saw at the organ recital where Bud made his debut."

"I inferred as much at the time. When are they to be married?"

"In June. Just as soon as the Annex can be added to the Jenkins's upright. They are to build on two new rooms or rather the Boarder will do so and he will furnish them for his new abiding-place. But because she is 'delicate like' and overworked she is to become a Boarderess instead of a housekeeper, and they will 'eat' with the Jenkins family, thus increasing the prosperity of the latter. Amarilly says the Boarder is 'awful gentle of Lily Rose and wants to take good care of her.'"

The expression that moved the frostiest of his flock came into the still depths of his eyes and brought the wild rose to Colette's cheeks.

"They are going to make quite an affair of the wedding," she continued, speaking hurriedly and a little breathlessly. "You and I and Mr. Phillips are to be guests. There is to be a hack to take the bride and groom to the train and a trip to Niagara Falls, because Lily Rose has never been on the cars. They are to have salad and ice-cream and sandwiches and coffee. Mr. Phillips is to act as florist and I shall furnish the decorations and the bride's bouquet. I'd love to throw in a bridal gown and veil, but Lily Rose, it seems, is proud and won't accept them."

"I can find it quite in my heart to admire the reluctance of Lily Rose to accept them."

"And so can I," replied Colette, the rare sweetness coming into her eyes. "Underneath all my jests about this wedding, it is all very sweet and touching to me—the Boarder's consideration for her, the preparations for the wedding which appear so elaborate to them. And then the wedding itself seems to mean so much to them. It's so different from the weddings in our class which often mean so little."

"Colette, I know—I have always known in spite of your endeavor to have me believe otherwise—anything really true and genuine appeals to you. I—"

"But I haven't told you yet," she said, seized with an unaccountable shyness, "what your part is to be. The Boarder, Lily Rose, and naturally all the Jenkinses, want you to perform the ceremony. The Boarder, being shy and retiring, forbore to ask you, and Amarilly for some reason desired me to ask you if you would officiate, and I assured her you would gladly do so."

"I should have felt hurt," replied John with a happy smile, "if they had asked anyone else to marry them. And you will be there, Colette?"

"Certainly," she declared. "I wouldn't miss it for anything."

"And—you will go with me, Colette?"

She colored, and her eyes drooped beneath his fixed gaze.

"Yes," she said, "I will go with you."

"Thank you, Colette," he answered gently, realizing what a surrender this was, and deeming it wise not to follow up his victory immediately.

And at his reticence Colette was conscious of a shade of disappointment. She began to feel an uncomfortable atmosphere in the silence that ensued, so she broke it, speaking hastily and confusedly.

"Oh, John, there is something else they want of you. The request is made by unanimous desire that you wear their surplice—that awful surplice!"

A shadow not unlike a frown fell athwart John's brow, and he made no immediate reply.

The introduction of the unfortunate topic made them both self-conscious, and for the first time Colette acknowledged to herself that she had been in the wrong in the matter of the surplice. John, misinterpreting her constraint, and fearing that the reference to the garment had revived all her old resentment, arose to depart.

"I will wear it if they wish," he said stiffly.

"I, too, wish you would wear it," she said in a voice scarcely audible.

He looked at her in surprise, hope returning.

"To please them," she added, coloring.

"Colette!" There was a pleading in his voice that told her all she longed to know. "Colette, don't you think I have been patient? Won't you be friends again?"

"I will," she said, "after—the Boarder's and Lily Rose's wedding!"

CHAPTER XXII

Work on the Boarder's Annex was begun with frantic zeal, each and every member of the Jenkins family lending a helping hand. The Boarder, as boss carpenter, worked after switching hours until it grew dark; then the children took turns, in holding a lantern for him. The savings of the Boarder being taxed by the trip to "Niagry" and the furnishing of the apartment, great economy had to be exercised in the erecting of the Annex. He strictly adhered to his determination not to touch the "rainy day fund."

Amarilly pleaded for a bay window, but the Boarder felt this ornamentation to be quite beyond his means, so they finally compromised on a small and simple porch on which Lily Rose could sit of a summer night while the Boarder smoked by her side. Mrs. Jenkins, moved to memories long dormant of the home of her youth, suggested blinds instead of window-shades, but the Boarder after much figuring proved adamantine in resistance to this temptation.

Lily Rose was the only one who made no suggestions. Anything the Boarder might construct in the way of a nesting place was beautiful in her eyes.

"She'd be too sorter modist-like to tell me if she was sot on any perticler thing about the new place," he confided wistfully to Amarilly, "You're so sharp I wish you'd kinder hint around and find out what she wants. Jest put out some feelers."

Amarilly diplomatically proceeded to put out "feelers," and after much maneuvering joyously imparted to the Boarder the information that Lily Rose loved to look at the one solitary tree that adorned the Jenkins lot, because to her it meant "the country."

"So that's the way she loves to look out," informed Amarilly, "and, you see there isn't any window on that side of your rooms."

"There shall be one," declared the Boarder firmly.

"Couldn't you make it a bay?" again coaxed Amarilly, "It's on the side the sun comes in most, and the doctor said Lily Rose should get all the sunlight she could. If she could sit in that bay window sunny days next winter it would be better than medicine for her."

The Boarder sighed.

"Don't tempt me, Amarilly. There ain't a cent more I kin squeeze out."

"I'll think out a way," thought Amarilly confidently.

She took the matter to Colette, who instantly and satisfactorily solved the problem, and Amarilly returned radiant.

"She says you've saved too much out for furniture, and to build the bay window from the furniture fund."

The Boarder shook his head.

"I thought of that, but thar ain't a thing I can take out of that. I got the figgers on the price of everything from the House Furnishers' Establishment."

"But you see, Miss King says no one ever comes to a wedding without bringing a present. That it wouldn't be et—,—dear me! I have forgotten what the word is. And she says not to buy any furniture till all the presents come, and then I can settle the rooms for you while you and Lily Rose are away. Lots of the things you are expecting to buy will be given you."

"It's risky," said the Boarder dubiously. "We'll most likely git casters and bibles and tidies. That's what I've allers seen to weddin's."

"Well, I see I have got to put a flea in your ear, but don't tell Lily Rose. Let it be a surprise to her. Miss King is going to give you a handsome base-burner coal stove. So you can take that off your list."

The Boarder looked pleased and yet distressed.

"She shouldn't go fer to do that!" he protested.

"Well, she wants to give you a nice present because you've been nice to us, and she thinks Lily Rose is sweet, and she says she believes in making sensible presents. She asked Mr. Meredith what to get, and he told her to get the stove so you see it's all right if he says so. She thought you wouldn't need a stove till next winter, but I told her you wanted the rooms furnished complete now."

"Then," said the Boarder beamingly, "the bay winder shall be cut out ter-morrer."

"Don't cut it out!" said Amarilly alarmed.

"I don't mean in a slang way," he said, laughing. "I mean cut out with a saw."

When Lily Rose was brought over one starlight night in budding May to see the beautiful aperture that would eventually become a bay window and face the solitary tree, two dewy drops of joy came into her eyes. Before them all she raised her pale, little face for a kiss which the Boarder bestowed with the solemn air of one pronouncing a benediction, for Lily Rose was chary of outward and visible expressions of affection, and he was deeply moved by this voluntary offering.

The Annex grew rapidly, but its uprising was not accomplished without some hazard and adventure. There was an exciting day when Cory fell through the scaffolding where she had been climbing. She suffered a moment of unconsciousness and a bump on her head.

"An inch nigher her brain, and it would have killed her!" exclaimed the mother in tragic tones.

"An inch of miss is as good as a mile," said the Boarder philosophically.

There was also a thrilling moment when Iry thrust his head through the railings of the new porch. Satisfied with his outlook, he would fain have withdrawn, but was prevented by an unaccountable swelling of his pate. Flamingus, coming to the rescue and working seemingly on the theory that his skull might be compressible, tried to pull him backward, but the frantic shrieks of Iry caused this plan of ejection to be abandoned.

"The rest of him is smaller than his head," observed Amarilly practically, as she arrived upon the scene and took a comprehensive view of the case, "Push him through, Flam, and I'll go around on the other side and get him."

Iry, safely landed in Amarilly's arms, laughed his delight, and thinking it a sort of game, was about to repeat his stunt of "in and out."

"It's time something was done to you," said Amarilly determinedly, "before you get killed in this place. I am going to spank you, Iry, and Co, too. I am going to spank you both fierce. And you are to keep away from the new part."

In spite of wailing protests, Amarilly administered a spanking to the two younger children that worked effectually against further repetition of their hazardous performances. But Bobby tobogganed down the roof during its shingling and sprained his ankle, which necessitated the use of crutches.

"He can break his neck if he wants to," remarked Amarilly, when besought by Co to punish him too.

Mrs. Jenkins lost a finger-nail by an injudicious use of the hammer. Bud sat down in the paint pot, and had to go to bed while his clothes were cleaned. In fact Lily Rose was the only one of the whole family circle to suffer no injury, but the Boarder guided her so tenderly over every part and plank of the Annex that there was no chance for mishap.

When the lathing and plastering were completed, the little bride-elect began to tremble with timidity and happiness at the consciousness of the nearness of her approaching transfer to the Home.

The plan of the Boarder had been to leave the walls rough and unfinished till their settling process should be accomplished, but Amarilly, absorbed heart and soul in this first experience of making a nesting place, pleaded for paper—"quiet, pretty paper with soft colors," she implored, Derry's teachings now beginning to bear fruit in Amarilly's development of the artistic.

"Amarilly, we can't hev everything to onct," he rebuked solemnly. "The paper'll crack as sure as fate, if you put it on now."

"Let it crack!" defied Amarilly. "Then you can put on more. You're away nearly all day, and the rest of us are at work, but if Lily Rose has to sit here all day and look at these white walls that look just like sour bread that hasn't riz"—Derry had not yet discovered this word in Amarilly's vocabulary—"she'll go mad."

"Amarilly," sighed the Boarder, "you'll hev me in the poorhouse yit!"

"Oh, dear!" sighed Amarilly. "I'll have to let you into another secret. Mr. Meredith is going to give you and Lily Rose a handsome centre-table and an easy-chair. There won't be any surprises left for you by the time the wedding is over, but you're so set, I have to keep giving things away to you."

"That makes me think," remarked the Boarder. "I was going to ask you what I'd orter give the preacher fer marryin' Lily Rose and me. The fireman of Number Six told me he give two dollars when he was spliced, but you see Mr. Meredith is so swell, I'd orter give more."

Amarilly gazed reflectively into space while she grappled with this proposition.

"Do you know," she said presently, with the rare insight that was her birthright, "I don't think Mr. Meredith would like money—not from you—for Lily Rose. You see he's a sort of a friend, and you'd better give him a present because money, unless it was a whole lot, wouldn't mean anything to him."

"That's so," admitted the Boarder, "but what kin I give him?"

Amarilly had another moment of thought.

"Make him a bookrack. Mr. Derry will draw you the design, and you can carve it out. You can do it noons after you eat your luncheon, then you won't lose any time building the house."

"That's jest what I'll do. So with the fee saved and the cheer and table out, I kin paper the rooms. You find out what kind Lily Rose wants and help her pick it out."

"She'll choose blue," lamented Amarilly, "and that fades quick."

Lily Rose was easily persuaded to let Derry be consulted. He promptly volunteered to tint the walls, having studied interior decorations at one time in his career. He wrought a marvellous effect in soft grays and browns with bordering graceful vines.

Lily Rose by taking advantage of a bargain sale on suits saved enough from her trousseau to curtain the windows in dainty blue and white muslin.

Derry then diverted the appropriation for an ingrain carpet to an expenditure for shellac and paint with which he showed Amarilly how to do the floors. Some cheap but pretty rugs were selected in place of the carpet.

At last the Annex was ready for painting. Lily Rose wistfully stated that she had always longed to live in a white house, so despite the fact that the Jenkins house proper was a sombre red, the new part was painted white.

"'Twill liven the place up," Amarilly consoled herself, while Colette breathed a sigh of relief that the Annex was not to be entirely conventional.

At Amarilly's suggestion, the woodwork was also painted white.

"Hard to keep clean," warned Amarilly, divided in her trend of practicality and her loyalty to St. John's favorite color. White won.

The moment the paint was dry and the Annex announced "done," the Boarder took Lily Rose to view their prospective domicile. They were unaccompanied by any of the family, but it took the combined efforts of Mrs. Jenkins, Amarilly, and Flamingus, whose recent change in voice and elongation of trousers gave him an air of authority, to prevent a stampede by the younger members.

Lily Rose returned wet-eyed, sweetly smiling, and tremulous of voice, but the Boarder stood erect, proud in his possessions.

Colette vetoed the plan for Amarilly to settle in the absence of the groom and bride.

"If you have it all furnished beforehand," she argued, "there will be just so much more room to entertain in on the night of the wedding."

And then Lily Rose confessed that "she'd love to be 'to hum' in her own place."

"But they won't be furnished," argued Amarilly.

"Oh, yes, they will," assured Colette. "It's etiquette—" she paused to note Amarilly writing the word down in a little book she carried—"for people to send their presents before they come, and you can settle as fast as they come in."

The wedding gifts all arrived the day before the wedding. The base-burner, though not needed for some months, was set up, because the Boarder said he would not feel at home until he could put his feet on his own hearth. John Meredith sent an oaken library table and an easy-chair. Derry's offering was in the shape of a beautiful picture and a vase for the table.

The best man, who fortunately had appealed to Amarilly for guidance, gave a couch. The Jenkins family, assessed in proportion to their respective incomes, provided a bedroom set. Lily Rose's landlady sent a willow rocker; the girl friends at the factory a gilt clock; the railroad hands, six silver spoons and an equal number of forks. Lily Rose's Sunday-school teacher presented a lamp. A heterogeneous assortment of articles came from the neighbors.

These presents were all arranged in the new rooms by Lily Rose, and the elegance of the new apartment was overwhelming in effect to the household.

"It looks most too fine to feel to hum in," gasped the Boarder. "It makes me feel strange!"

"It won't look strange to you," assured the bride-elect, looking shyly into his adoring eyes, "when you come home and find me sitting here in my blue dress waiting for you, will it?"

"No!" agreed the Boarder with a quick intake of breath, "'Twill be home and heaven, Lily Rose."

CHAPTER XXIII

Shyly and perversely Lily Rose had postponed the trying on of her borrowed wedding waist until the day preceding the great event.

"There won't be time to fit it," pleaded Amarilly.

And Lily Rose had smiled a faraway smile and said her veil would cover it anyway. But finally Amarilly's pleas prevailed and the beloved garment was brought forth.

Amarilly took it reverently from its wrappings and held it up to view. After many exclamations of wonder and admiration, Lily Rose, who had removed her dress, essayed to try it on.

"Why, Amarilly," she said, struggling to get her arm into the sleeve, "there's something the matter! It's sewed together, or something."

Amarilly hastened to investigate.

"Oh!" she gasped, after thrusting her hand within, "to think it should be in here, for I am sure this is what Miss King has been looking for so long. Wait until I go and ask ma about it."

She hurried to the kitchen precinct of the house.

"Oh, Ma, do you know how this came in Miss King's lace waist? The one that was here through the fever?"

"Why, didn't you ever take that home?"

"Yes," informed Amarilly, "but she made me a present of it, and I put it away to keep till I was — grown up. And I want to lend it to Lily Rose to be married in. And when she went to try it on, she found this in the sleeve."

Mrs. Jenkins paused in the sudsing of a garment.

"Let me see!" she said, surveying the object with reminiscent scrutiny. "Oh, yes, I remember now. I found it on the floor the day she was here, afore the waist was ready for her. I thought she had dropped it, and so I pinned it in the sleeve of her dress, and was goin to tell Gus to give it to her, but he didn't take the waist hum, and then so much happened, it went clean out of my mind."

"I'll go right over to her house with it now," said Amarilly.

Lily Rose, adorned in the filmy, white waist, entered the kitchen.

"See, Amarilly," she said delightedly. "It's a beautiful fit!"

But Amarilly had something on her mind of more moment even than Lily Rose's wedding garments.

"I am glad it fits," she said hurriedly, scarcely vouchsafing a glance toward Lily Rose as she caught up her hat, and hastened as fast as the street-cars would take her to Colette. Orders had been given for the admittance of Amarilly at any hour and to any room her young patroness might chance to be occupying. This morning she was in her boudoir.

"Oh, Miss King!" cried Amarilly, her face aglow. "I guess I have found it!"

Colette's heart began to flutter and the wavering beat became a steady throb when Amarilly handed her the long lost article.

"Oh, Amarilly, you darling! Yes, yes, this is it! And it evidently has not been touched. Where did you find it? Who had it?" Amarilly related the story of its discovery.

"Then, but for your generosity, Amarilly, this would have been in the waist for years, so I am going to reward you. You shall make Lily Rose a wedding present of the waist, and when you are married, I shall give you a real, white wedding gown of white satin with a bridal train!"

"Oh, Miss King! I must get married then, even if I have to do it in a leap year!"

"Of course you will marry. I shall pick out the bridegroom myself. I feel like doing almost anything for you, Amarilly."

"Do you, truly?" asked Amarilly. "Then I wish you would—"

"Tell me, dear!" urged Colette. "I'll do anything for you to-day."

"Be nice to Mr. St. John!" whispered the little peacemaker.

"Amarilly! I will, indeed—nicer than you can imagine, or he either. And tell me, is Lily Rose still happy—very happy?"

"Yes," replied Amarilly. "So happy, and so scared-like, and she's going to dress at our house and could you come early and fix on the veil? We don't just know how it goes."

"Of course I will. And now will you take a little note to St. John for me on your way home?"

"Yes, Miss King. And are you going to tell him it is found?"

"No, Amarilly; not until to-morrow night, so don't say anything about it to him."

The rector looked up with a welcoming smile when Amarilly was shown into his study.

"I came with a note from her," she said with a glad little intonation in her voice.

John took it eagerly. His face fell at the first few words which told him not to call for her to-morrow night on the way to the wedding, but it brightened amazingly when he read the reason—the adjusting of Lily Rose's bridal veil; it fairly radiated joy when he read:

"I am not going to be disagreeable to—anyone to-morrow. I shall 'let my light shine' on Lily Rose and—every one. If you will keep your carriage to-morrow night, I will send mine away and ride home with you."

CHAPTER XXIV

On the night of the auspicious occasion, Mrs. Jenkins's home presented a scene of festivity. Neighbors had loaned their lamps, and the brakeman had hung out his red lantern in token of welcome and cheer. It was, however, mistaken by some of the guests as a signal of danger, and they were wary of their steps lest they be ditched. Mrs. Hudgers ventured the awful prognostication that "mebby some of them Jenkins brats had gone and got another of them ketchin' diseases."

When they entered the house there was a general exclamation of admiration. The curtain partitions had been removed, and the big room was beautifully decorated with festoons and masses of green interspersed with huge bunches of June roses.

Derry and Flamingus received the guests. Upstairs the Boarder and the brakeman were nervously awaiting the crucial moment. The door into the Annex was closed, for in the sitting-room was the little bride, her pale cheeks delicately tinted from excitement as Colette artistically adjusted the bridal veil, fastening it with real orange blossoms. Amarilly hovered near in an ecstasy which was perforce silent on account of her mouth being full of pins.

"There's Mr. St. John's carriage," she managed to murmur as she peered from the window.

Colette dropped her paper of pins, went hastily into the adjoining bedroom and slipped out again before John Meredith was ushered in where the surplice immaculately laundered, was waiting to be donned by its original owner.

After slipping it on, John's hand from force of habit sought the pocket and there encountered something. He drew it forth wonderingly. It was a small, silver-monogrammed envelope sealed and addressed to him in Colette's handwriting. He read the note once, twice, thrice. Then there was a knock at the door that led into the Annex sitting-room. He opened it to admit Amarilly.

"Are you ready?" she asked. "You're to go in with them. They —"

She paused and stared at him. The transformation in his face was wonderful.

"Yes, I am ready, Amarilly," he replied, and something in his voice sounded strange to her.

He followed her into the next room where the Boarder, awkward in his Sunday clothes, but regal in his pride in the little, white-veiled figure at his side, was awaiting him.

John walked out into the Jenkins's part of the house with them, while

Amarilly slipped home by way of the Annex bedroom.

The entrance was certainly effective to the neighbors.

"Ain't she a lily though!" "Look at that long veil onct!" "Jest like 'a picter!" "What a swell waist" "That big bo'quet!" "I niver seed sech flowers afore." "That surplus makes it look like picters!"

All these comments were sweet music in Amarilly's ear. Only one person had regrets. Mrs. Hudgers was visibly disappointed.

"I thought they'd hev candles a-burnin'," she confided to Mrs. Huce.

"Don't you know no better than that?" scoffed Mrs. Huce with a superior air. "Them things is only used by Irish folks."

Derry's dancing eyes looked to Colette for appreciation of this statement, but her eyes and attention were entirely for John.

The ceremony began. John's impressive voice, with its new pervading note of exultant gladness, reached them all, tempering even Derry's light-hearted mirth. It gave courage to the little bride whose drooping head rose like a flower, and a light shone in her eyes as she made the responses sweetly and clearly. It found echo in the Boarder, whose stooping shoulders unconsciously straightened and his voice grew clear and strong as he promised to have and to hold. It found a place in Colette's heart which sent illumining lights into her starry eyes.

When the solemn ceremony ended, and the Boarder and Lilly Rose were pronounced man and wife, the guests flocked forward to offer congratulations. Then they were bidden to adjourn to the Annex that they might view the bride's domain, while Mrs. Jenkins assisted by many helping hands set the long tables, a small one being reserved for the Boarder, the bride, Mr. Cotter, and Mrs. Jenkins and Iry.

"I thought they could eat more natural," whispered the considerate little Amarilly to Colette, "if there weren't no strangers with them."

Colette, John, and Derry were also honored with a separate table. Mrs. Hudgers and Amarilly "dished up and poured" in the woodshed, while the boys acted as waiters, having been thoroughly trained by Amarilly for the occasion.

"Do you know," laughed Derry, "I was so surprised and relieved to find that the Boarder had a cognomen like other people. It never occurred to me before that he must of course have a name."

Colette smiled politely but perfunctorily. She was living too deeply to-night to appreciate wit. John, too, was strangely silent, his eyes resting often and adoringly upon Colette. Shrewdly Derry divined the situation and relieved it by rattling on with a surface banter that demanded no response.

"These refreshments," he observed, "are certainly the handiwork of my little maid. They have a flavor all her own. I am proud of Amarilly's English, too."

"I wonder," said Colette, "if you are doing quite right, Mr. Phillips, in improving Amarilly to such an extent? I am afraid she will grow beyond her family."

"No; even you, pardon me, Miss King, don't know Amarilly as I do. She couldn't get beyond them in her heart, although she may in other directions. Her heart is in the right place, and it will bridge any distance that may lie between them."

John looked up attentively and approvingly.

"Amarilly has too much aptitude for learning not to be encouraged, and I shall do more for her before long. We have pursued a select course of reading this winter. She has read aloud while I painted. We began stumblingly with Alice in Wonderland and are now groping through mythology."

After refreshments had been served, Lily Rose went to her bedroom to don her travelling gown, and when the happy couple had driven away amid a shower of rice and shouts from the neighbors, John's carriage drew up.

"John," asked Colette, after a happy little moment in his arms, "did you read my note and did you see what the date was?"

"Colette, surely it was the dearest love-letter a man ever received. If

I could have had it all these dreary months!"

"Do you wonder that I feared its falling into strange hands?"

"Tell me its history, Colette. How you recovered it, and why you thought it was in the surplice in the first place?"

"I wrote it the day after you asked me—you know—"

There was another happy disappearance and silence before she resumed:

"I was sentimental enough to want to deliver it in an unusual way. I took it to Mrs. Jenkins's house the day your surplice was to be returned to you, and I slipped it inside the pocket. I wanted you to find it there on Sunday morning. I didn't know what to think when you looked at me so oddly that Sunday—yes, I know now that you were wondering at my silence. And when we came home in the fall and I learned from Amarilly that strangers might be reading and laughing at my ardent love-letter, which must have passed through many and alien hands, I was so horrified I couldn't act rational or natural. I was—yes, I will 'fess up, John,— I was unreasonable, as you said and—No, John! wait until I finish before you—"

"You want to know how and where it was found? It seems at the same time your surplice was laundered, a lace waist of mine was at their house. I didn't care for a 'fumigated waist' so, like you, I made Amarilly a present perforce. She laid it away in its wrappings to keep until her wedding day. Out of the goodness of her generous little heart she loaned it to Lily Rose and yesterday, when they were trying it on, Amarilly found my note in the sleeve. Mrs. Jenkins was appealed to and remembered that when the things were ready to be sent home, she found the note on the floor, and supposing it had fallen from the waist slipped it inside and forgot all about it. I decided that it should be delivered in the manner originally planned."

"But, Colette," he asked wistfully, a few moments later, "if you had never found it would you have kept me always in suspense and never have given me an answer? I began to hope, that night I called, that you were relenting."

"I was, John. Amarilly had been telling me of the Boarder's love for Lily Rose, and it made me lonely for you, and I determined in any event to give you your answer—this answer—to-night. And so I did, and—I think that is all, John."

"Not all, Colette."

CHAPTER XXV

The dairy business continued to prove profitable to Gus, the cow remaining contented, loving and giving. One night, however, there came the inevitable reaction, and the gentle creature in the cow-shed felt the same stifling she had rebelled against on the night of the stampede when she had made her wild dash for liberty. Moved by these recollections, the sedate, orderly cow became imbued with a feeling of unrest, and demolishing the frail door was once more at large. In a frenzy of freedom she dashed about the yard. Her progress was somewhat impeded by contact with the surplice which, pinned to the clothes-line, was flapping in the breezes. Maddened by this obstruction which hung, veil-like, over her bovine lineaments, she gave a twist of her Texas horns, a tug, and the surplice was released, but from the line only; it twined itself like a white wraith about the horns.

Then the sportive animal frisked over the low back fence and across the hill, occasionally stepping on a released end of the surplice and angrily tearing her way through the garment. She made her road to the railroad track. That sight, awakening bitter memories of a packed cattle-car, caused her to slacken her Mazeppa-like speed. While she paused, the night express backed onto the side track to await the coming of the eastbound train. The cow, still in meditation, was silhouetted in the light of a harvest moon.

"This 'ere," a home-bound cattleman was saying to a friend on the platform, "is nigh onto whar we dropped a cow. I swar if thar ain't that blasted cow now, what? Know her from hoof to horn, though what kind of a Christmas tree she's got on fer a bunnit, gits me! Ki, yi! Ki, yi!"

At the sound of the shrill, weird cry, the animal stood at bay. Again came the well-known strident halloo. A maelstrom of memories was awakened by the call. Instinctively obeying the old summons she started toward the train, when from over the hill behind her she heard another command.

"Co, boss! Co, boss!"

The childish anxious treble rose in an imploring wail.

150

The cow paused irresolute, hesitating between the lure of the old life on the plains and the recent domestic existence.

"Co, boss!"

There was a note of entreaty, of affection, in the cry.

After all, domesticity was her birthright. With an answering low of encouragement the black cow turned and trotted amiably back to meet the little dairyman.

"Well, I'll be jiggered," said the cattleman, as the train pulled out. "I'd a swore it was old Jetblack. Maybe 'twas. She was only a milker anyway, and I guess she's found a home somewhere."

Gus with arm lovingly about the cow's neck walked home.

"Bossy," he said in gently reproaching tones, "how could you give me such a skeer? I thought I'd lost you, and I'd hev sure missed you — you, yerself — more'n I would the money your milk brings us."

Then for the first time, the lad's eyes noted the decorated horns.

"What in thunder — "

He began to unwind the ribbons of white cloth, the stringed remnants of the surplice.

"Gracious Peter! It's the surplus! What will Amarilly say — and Lily Rose? It's only fit fer carpet rags now. Well, if this ain't the end of the surplus after all it has went through! I wonder what bossy wanted of it? Thought jest cause she was a cow, she must be a cow ketcher, I suppose."

Great was the joy of the Jenkinses at the restoration of the cow, but there was grievous lament from Amarilly for the fate of the precious garment.

"It was our friend — our friend in need!" she mourned.

"I'm so glad we hev a picter of it," said Lily Rose, gazing fondly at the photograph of the Boarder in the saintly robes.

"I'll go and tell Miss King," said Amarilly the next morning. "She said she felt that the surplice would come to some tragic end."

"It was a fitting fate for so mysterious a garment," commented Colette. "You couldn't expect any ordinary, common-place ending for the surplice. After officiating at funerals, weddings, shop-windows, theatres, pawnshops, and bishops' dwellings, it could never have simply worn out, or died of old age."

"I don't see," meditated Amarilly, "what possessed the cow. She's been so gentle always, and then to fly to pieces that way, and riddle the surplice to bits! It was lucky there was nothing else on the line."

"It's very simple," said Colette. "I suppose she wanted to go to the train. Maybe she expected to meet a friend. And as nearly everyone else had worn the surplice on special occasions, she thought she could do the same; only, you see, never having been to church she didn't quite know how to put it on, and I suppose got mad at it because it didn't fit her and gave vent to her anger by trampling on it."

Amarilly's doleful little face showed no appreciation of this conceit.

"Don't look so glum, Amarilly. I have something to show you that will please you."

She opened a desk and took a thick, white square envelope from it, and handed it to the little girl.

Wonderingly Amarilly opened it and took out a folded, engraved sheet of thick paper. She read eagerly, and two little spots of pink came into her cheeks.

"Oh, oh!" she cried, looking up with shining eyes, which in another moment glistened through tears.

"Why, Amarilly, aren't you glad that I am going to be — "

"Mrs. St. John?" smiled Amarilly. "I think it's beautiful. And," anxiously, "you will surely be good to — him?"

"Yes," replied Colette softly "I will be good — very good — to St. John.

Don't fear, Amarilly."

A card had fallen from the envelope. Amarilly picked it up and read:

"To be presented at the church."

"What's that?" she asked curiously.

"You have to show that at the church door. If you didn't have it, you couldn't get in to see us married. It's the same as a ticket to a theatre. And St. John doesn't like it; but if we didn't have them there would be a mob of curious people who don't know us. I shall give all of you tickets to come to the church, the Boarder and Lily Rose, too."

"Oh," cried Amarilly, "that will be lovely, and we shall all come."

"Of course you will all come. Your friend, the bishop, is to marry us, and Bud is going to sing a solo. The choirmaster told me his voice was developing wonderfully."

"I must go home and tell them all about it," said Amarilly excitedly.

"Wait! There's more to hear. I am going to invite you to the reception here at the house, and I am going to have a lovely white dress made for you to wear, and you shall have white silk stockings and slippers and white gloves."

"Oh!" gasped Amarilly, shutting her eyes. "I can't believe it."

The next morning at the studio she announced the wonderful news to Derry.

"I just received an invitation, myself," he replied. "We will go together, Amarilly. I'll send you flowers and call for you with a taxicab."

"Things must stop happening to me," said Amarilly solemnly. "I can't stand much more."

Derry laughed.

"When things once begin to happen, Amarilly, they never stop. You are to go from here now every day after luncheon to this address," handing her a card.

"'Miss Varley,'" Amarilly read. "'1227, Winter Street.' Will she have work for me, too?"

"Yes; work in schoolbooks. She takes a few private pupils, and I have engaged her to teach you. I really think you should have instruction in other branches than English and art and arithmetic."

Amarilly turned pale but said nothing for a moment. Then she held out her hand.

"I will study hard—to pay you," she said simply.

"And can you stand another piece of exciting news, Amarilly? Sunset, which I have dawdled over for so long, drew first prize."

"Oh, Mr. Derry, that is best of all!"

"And do you know what I am going to give Mrs. St. John for a wedding present from you and me? The picture of The Little Scrub-girl."

CHAPTER XXVI

Another spring found the members of the Jenkins Syndicate still banking regularly and flourishing in their various walks in life. The Boarder had received a "raise"; Lily Rose was spending her leisure time in fashioning tiny garments which she told Cory were for a doll baby; Iry was wearing his first trousers cut over from a pair discarded by Bud; and Amarilly was acquiring book lore with an ease and rapidity which delighted Miss Varley and Derry. Through the medium of Mr. Vedder the attention of the manager of a high class vaudeville had been drawn to Bud, and he was now singing every night with a salary that made the neighbors declare that "them Jenkinses was getting to be reg'ler Rockyfellers."

Amarilly coming home one Monday evening found the family grouped about the long table listening with bulging eyes and hectic cheeks to the Boarder, who had before him a sheet of figures. Amarilly was at once alert, although somewhat resentful of this encroachment upon her particular province.

"Oh, come and hear, Amarilly!" "Amarilly, we've bought a farm!"

"Amarilly, we air agoin' to live in the country!"

"Let me explain," said the Boarder, usually slow and easy going, but now alert and enthusiastic of mien and speech. "We've got a chance, Amarilly, to sell this place and make quite a profit. That new factory that's agoin' up acrost the alley has sent real estate scootin'. With what we git fer it, we kin make a big payment on a farm. I took a run down yesterday to look at one we kin git cheap, cause the folks on it hez gotter go west fer the man's health. What we hev all saved up sence we bought the place will keep us agoin' till we git in our fust summer crops."

"Tell her about the house," prompted Mrs. Jenkins, her quick, maternal eye noting the bewilderment and disapproval in her daughter's expressive eyes.

"It's all green meaders and orcherds and lanes," said the Boarder with the volubility of one repeating an oft-told and well-loved tale, while the young Jenkinses with the rapt, intense gaze of moving picture beholders sat in pleased expectancy, "and the house sets on a little rise of ground. It's a white house with a big chimbley and two stoops, and thar's a big barn with two white hosses in it, and a cow and an animal in the paster lot. A big pen of pigs, fifty hens in the henhouse, and a few sheep. Thar's a piece of woods and the river."

"I'm a little fearful of the river on Iry's account," said Mrs. Jenkins, "but we kin spank him up good as soon as we git thar, and then he'll understand he's to keep away."

"We kin git a good dog to keep track of Iry and the cattle," said the Boarder, and then he paused expectantly to listen to Amarilly's approbation. But she was strangely silent.

"It will be a fust class investment," he continued sagely.

"Why will it? We don't know anything about farming," objected Amarilly.

"We'll have to hire someone to run it."

"I was brought up on a farm," replied the Boarder. "Thar ain't a thing I don't know about farm work."

"I was raised on a farm, too," said Mrs. Jenkins. "I can make good butter and I know all about raisin' chickens. I'll get some young turkeys and have them ready to sell for Thanksgiving, and I'll set out strawberries and celery plants."

"I kin larn, and I'll work hard and do just what he tells me to," said

Flamingus, motioning toward the Boarder.

"I kin have my dairy all right, all right," said Gus joyfully. "I'll have a hull herd of cattle soon."

"I shall go in heavy on hens," said Milt importantly. "The grocer give me a book about raising them. There's money in hens."

"I choose to take keer of the sheep," cried Bobby.

"I'll help ma do the work in the house and the garden," volunteered

Cory.

"And I'm strong enough to work outdoors now," said Lily Rose. "I shall help with the garden and with the housework."

"We'll all pitch in and work," said Flamingus authoritatively, "and we're all partners and we won't hire no help. It will be clear profit."

"Ain't it lovely, Amarilly?" asked the mother, apprehensive lest the little leader might blackball the project.

"We're all doing so well here, why change? Why not let well enough alone?" she asked.

There was a general and surprised protest at this statement. It was something new for Amarilly to be a kill-joy.

"Do you like to live in this alley when we kin hev all outdoors and git a chanst to be somebody?" demanded Flamingus, who was rapidly usurping his sister's place as head of the house.

"And think of the money we'll make!" reminded Milton.

"And the milk and butter and cream and good things to eat without buying them!" exclaimed Gus.

"And huntin' f'r eggs and swimmin' in the river and skatin' and gettin' hickory nuts and all the apples you kin eat," persuaded Bobby, who had evidently been listening to the Boarder's fancies of farm life.

"Thar's a school close by, and all the chillern kin go," said the mother anxiously. "Mebby you kin git to teach it after a while, Amarilly."

"Oh, Amarilly!" cried Lily Rose ecstatically, "to think of all the trees, and all the sky, and all the green grass and all the birds—oh, Amarilly!"

Words failed Lily Rose, but she sighed a far-seeing blissful sigh of exquisite happiness at her horoscope. The Boarder looked at her, his heart eloquent in his eyes, but he said nothing.

"Amarilly," cried Cory, "we kin hev real flowers fer nuthin' and pies and ice-cream, and we kin cuddle little chicks like ma told me, and make daisy chains, and hev picnics in the woods. Oh—"

Words also proved inadequate to Co's anticipations.

"Amawilly, we kin play wiv little lambs," lisped Iry.

"Bud, you haven't made your speech, yet," said Amarilly, wistfully, realizing that the majority was against her.

"Bud won't go till fall," said Mrs. Jenkins.

"Till fall!" cried Amarilly faintly. "Why, when are we going?"

"Next week," answered the Boarder jubilantly. "The folks want to leave right away, and we must get busy plantin'. I went to Vedder's friend, the real estate man, this mornin' as soon as I got back, and he says it's a real bargain."

"But why isn't Bud going?"

"This morning," informed Mrs. Jenkins proudly, "Bud had an offer. As soon as the theatre shuts down, Mr. Vedder is going to take Bud to a big resort and manage him for the season. He'll git lots of money. I wouldn't let Bud go off with no one else, but Mr. Vedder is so nice, and he says when Bud goes to the country in the fall he kin come into the city Saturday nights on the Interurban and sing in the choir Sundays and come back Monday. He kin stay with him, Mr. Vedder says. And the country air and the fresh milk and eggs, will make a diff'rent boy of him. It's what the doctor says he'd orter hev."

"Then, we'll go, of course," declared Amarilly resolutely.

"And, Amarilly," said the Boarder gravely, "your ma ain't said why she wanted to go, but think of the diff'rence it will make in her life. To be sure, she will have to work hard, but with you, Lily Rose, and Co to help her, it won't be so hard, and it'll be higher class work than slushing around in tubs and water, and she'll hev good feedin' and good air, and we'll all feel like we was folks and our own bosses."

"Ma, I was selfish!" cried Amarilly remorsefully. "I'll work like a hired man!"

Amarilly thereupon bravely assumed a cheerful mien and looked over the Boarder's figures, listening with apparently great enthusiasm to the plans and projects. But when she was upstairs in her own little bed and each and every other Jenkins was wrapt in happy slumber, she turned her face to the wall, and wept long, silently, and miserably. Far-away fields and pastures did not look alluring to this little daughter of the city who put bricks and mortar and lighted streets above trees and meadows, for Amarilly was entirely metropolitan; sky-scrapers were her birthright, and she loved every inch of her city.

"But it's best for them," she acknowledged.

A little pang came with the realization that they who had been so dependent upon her guardianship for guidance were entirely competent to act without her.

"It's Flam. He's growed up!" she sobbed, correctness of speech slipping from her in her grief. "And he don't know near so much as I do, only he's a man — or going to be — so what he says goes."

And with this bitter but inevitable recognition of the things that are,

Amarilly sobbed herself to sleep.

CHAPTER XXVII

The next morning Amarilly served Derry's breakfast in heavy-hearted silence, replying in low-voiced monosyllables to his gay, conversational advances. She performed her household duties about the studio listlessly though with conscientious thoroughness. When it came time to prepare luncheon, Derry called her into the studio.

"Come here to the light, where I can see you best, Amarilly."

Reluctantly she came.

He turned his searching, artist's eyes upon her unsparingly, noting the violet shadows under the white-lidded eyes, and the hard, almost tragic lines in the drooping of her mobile mouth. She bore his gaze unflinchingly, with indrawn breath and clenched hands.

"What is it, Amarilly?" he asked gently. "You will tell me, nicht wahr?"

These two last words were in deference to her new study of German.

At the genuine sympathy in his voice, Amarilly's composure gave way and there was a rush of tears.

He led her to a divan and sat beside her.

"Yes, of course you will tell me, Amarilly. I knew there was an emotional side to my practical, little maid, and I noticed at breakfast that there was something wrong."

"Yes," she replied, with an effort, wiping away the rising tears, "I will tell you, but no one else. If I told Mr. Vedder, he would not understand; he would say I must do what was sensible. If I told Mr. St. John, he would be shocked, and tell me that duty was hard, and that was why it must be done,—to strengthen. Mrs. St. John would laugh, and say: 'Oh, what a foolish Amarilly!'"

"And what will I say, Amarilly?" he asked interestedly.

"You! Oh, you will understand what I feel, and you will be sorry."

"Then spin away, Amarilly. You'll have my sympathy and help in everything that makes you feel bad, whether it's right or wrong."

"Oh, Mr. Derry, we are all going away — way off to the country — to live on a farm!"

"Amarilly, you little city brat! You'd be a misfit on a farm. Tell me what has sent the Jenkins family into the open."

Faithfully Amarilly enumerated the pros and cons of the agricultural venture. When she had concluded her narrative, Derry, to her surprise and sorrow, looked positively jubilant.

"And you don't want to live in the country, eh, Amarilly?"

"No, Mr. Derry," she protested. "I don't. I have never been there, but I know the woods and the fields and — all that — must be beautiful — in patches — but I couldn't bear it all the time — not to see all the bright and white lights at night and the hurry, and the people, and the theatres. No! I'd rather be the poorest little speck here than to own and live on the biggest farm in the world."

He laughed delightedly.

"Oh, Amarilly, you little gamin! You have the right idea, though. We don't want anything, however perfect it may be, all the time. We want it just 'in patches' — as you say. You'll love the country with your whole heart and soul when you come to see it if you know that you can leave it. But this is a big change in your affairs, and we must talk it over. We'll go to Carter's again for luncheon. Take off your apron and cap. You won't have to fix your hair this time. It's even more beautiful than it was then. Your frock, if it is cheap and plain, is artistic in cut and color."

Amarilly felt cheered in spite of herself at his exuberant manner, but burst into tears when on leaving the studio he casually remarked:

"So this is almost the last of your work here! I can never hope to get such another housekeeper as you. I shall have to eat out again."

At sight of her grief he took hold of her arm almost roughly.

"Amarilly, you little goose, do you suppose I am going to let you be exiled to a farm and lapse into the vernacular of the Boarder? Now, buck up and trust to the judgment and affection of your twin brother."

Amarilly, wondering but hopeful, "bucked up," and they walked in silence to Carter's, where Derry ordered a private dining-room and luncheon. Then:

"Now, listen my child, and you shall hear, not of the midnight ride of Paul Revere, but of the sad story of the life of your twin brother. My parents died when I was too young to grieve for them. They are only a faint memory. I had a cold-blooded, sensible guardian who put me into a boys' school, from which I went to college, and then for a year in Paris. He didn't let me know the amount of my inheritance. Consequently I really worked and worked hard at the only thing I cared for and formed no extravagant tastes. Neither was I courted and flattered by parasites.

"On my return from Paris, a year before I met you, I came into my mother's fortune, and recently I have received the one left me by my father. Having been brought up to live a comparatively simple life, in the belief that I would be dependent on my own exertions, I have more money than I know what to do with as yet. I have no one, not even a fifth cousin, to be interested in. I have any number of acquaintances, but no really intimate friends, so I have no one to help me spend and enjoy my money.

"There was something about you, Amarilly, that appealed to me that first day you came up to the studio. It couldn't have been your looks, for aside from your hair, your expressive eyes, and your hands; you are quite ordinary looking; but something about you amused me, then interested me, and, now fascinates me. I have thought about it a good deal, and have come to the conclusion that it is your direct naturalness and earnestness. I have really come to feel as if you were a sort of a younger sister of mine. I have done a very little for you in the way of education, and I have intended to do more. The reason I have been slow about it was—for reasons. I have discussed your future with the Merediths a great many times.

"What I wished to do was to put you in the best girls' school I could find and when you were finished there, to send you abroad, and give you the same advantages that a sister of mine would have. But as I say, I hesitated. It didn't seem exactly wise to separate you from your family, surround you with different environments and then have you come home to—the alley. I know your loyal little heart would never waver in its affection for them, but such a decided change would not be wise.

"Now, you see, this farm business simplifies things wonderfully. With the thrift and industry of your brothers and the Boarder I can easily see the farm is going to be a prosperous undertaking, and by the time you are finished—say five years—for Miss Varley tells me you are quite up with the girls of your age in your studies, they will have a substantial country home which you will enjoy immensely between times. You will find that a country home, however humble, is not sordid like an obscure home in the city. So next week, Amarilly, or as soon as Mrs. Meredith can fit you out properly, you will be packed off to an ultra- smart school. There will be one term this year, but I think you should remain through the summer vacation and have private tutoring."

The waiter entered with the first course. When he had again gone out, Amarilly looked up at Derry, her eyes full of a yearning that touched him.

"It would be lovely, Mr. Derry. Too lovely to happen, you know."

"There, Amarilly," he said with a combination of frown and smile, "there it is again—your contradiction of eyes and mouth—the one of a gazelle; the other, of a mule. I'll answer your objections before you make them, for it is determined that you are to go."

The look he had ascribed to Amarilly's mouth came into the forward thrust of his chin.

"First, you think you are too proud and independent to accept. From your viewpoint it seems a good deal to do. From mine, proved by my bank account, it is an absurdly small thing to do, but if you are truly grateful for what you are pleased to think I have done for you, you will let me do this, because you feel sorry for me that I am so alone in the world. And St. John, himself, would tell you it was your duty to make the most of your talents and opportunities. You can also do a little charity work in keeping me straight, for you see, Amarilly, I am going to Paris for two years to study, and I will have an incentive to work and not play too hard if I know I have a little sister over here in school who would be sorry if her brother went wrong and didn't get to be a great artist. So for your sake, and for my sake—"

"But there's ma's sake," she said wistfully. "The Boarder says woman's work on the farm is hard."

"There's the Boarderess and Co—"

"Lily Rose is not strong and doesn't know much about farm work, and Co's only a kid."

"Well, I hadn't finished. You have an interest in the farm as one of the syndicate, and you have some money saved."

"Yes," admitted Amarilly bewildered, not following his train of thought.

"Well, you won't need that now, and it can go towards a woman to help,— a hired girl in country vernacular—during the busy seasons. And you can go home summers. Every week you are to write me a long letter and tell me about yourself and them."

Amarilly was gazing into space, and in silence he watched the odd, little signs of conflict. It was the same sort of a struggle, only harder and more prolonged, that she had passed through two years before at the theatre when her untutored conscience bade her relinquish her seat. Suddenly her countenance became illumined.

"I am going to do it, Mr. Derry! I am going to let you send me to school, and abroad and wherever you think best."

THE END

Milton Keynes UK
Ingram Content Group UK Ltd.
UKHW010857040923
428018UK00004B/388

9 791041 829842